# AVOIDABLE HARM

## *WHEN THE BOTTOM LINE IS ALL THAT MATTERS*

## TONY SCLAMA

Tony Sclama Books

This is a work of fiction. Names, characters, places, and incidents either are the product of the author's imagination, or are used fictitiously. Any resemblance to actual persons, living or dead, events, organizations, or locales, is entirely coincidental.



First paperback edition 2023
Published by Tony Sclama Books
www.tonysclama.com

ISBN 978-1-7372656-3-4

Cover and Interior Design by Ebook Launch

# CHAPTER ONE

It was nearly midnight. The man was bleary-eyed as he walked home from work in downtown Baltimore, and he didn't notice the woman on the ledge.

Until the glint of light from the window high above beckoned him to look up.

He wasn't even sure it was a woman.

Until he squinted, adjusting his eyes to the surrounding darkness.

And she wasn't really standing on the ledge—just straddling the sill of the open window.

Until she swung her leg over.

And then she jumped.

# CHAPTER TWO

Megan bolted upright from sleep in a cold sweat, eyes wide, breathing heavily.

The nightmarish reenactment of her brief but frightening captivity by an armed assailant was almost a nightly occurrence since the horrific event more than a year ago. She and her aunt, Allisyn McLoren, surely would have been killed by a biotech firm's henchman as part of its conspiracy to defraud the government if not for the timely intervention of an FBI agent.

She had been able to come to terms with its finality and suppress thoughts of it when awake but couldn't prevent sleep from dredging up the terrible event from the deepest level of her psyche.

After completing her medical residency in D.C. several months earlier, Megan was accepted for a highly sought-after fellowship in Infectious Disease and research at a prestigious university hospital in Boston that was not to start for another year. Since she was required to complete one preliminary year of hospital-based clinical patient care, she accepted a job as a hospitalist physician in a less metropolitan setting, hoping for a broader perspective on healthcare than her time in Washington.

Wallberg General Hospital, often referred to as WGH, was a not-for-profit community hospital and namesake of the western Massachusetts city where it was located.

Now, after two months, WGH Medical Director Art Kinkaid had asked to meet with her to see how she was adjusting to the workload. She glanced at the bedside clock and sighed. It was still three hours before her 7:00 a.m. meeting, and it would take her only ten minutes to reach the hospital from the small apartment she was temporarily renting.

She slowly rolled out of bed and grimaced at the still dark view out her window. After showering, she dressed and grabbed her white jacket, stethoscope in tow, and a travel mug of coffee for the ride, hoping a space in the usually crowded employee parking area would be readily accessible this early.

# CHAPTER THREE

"What the hell is this?" asked WGH Board Chair Elsbeth Sentini as she burst into the executive suite office of Alan Fresney, hospital CEO. Sentini was waving the hospital's most recent financial report in advance of an upcoming meeting of the full board. She approached his desk and slammed the document down. "This is unacceptable, Alan."

"Easy, Elsbeth," said Fresney. "Calm down."

"Calm down? Seriously? Do you think the other board members are going to feel any differently? Not to mention our donors. Need I remind you their significant contributions were the result of my efforts? Not an easy task given the hospital's previous financial performance was only marginally worse than this."

The CEO frowned. "Let me explain—"

"Don't bother. It's my reputation and credibility at stake with the donors, not yours. Just be prepared at the meeting with your plan to fix this mess." She turned abruptly to leave. "And it better be good," she added, looking back at him as she exited, slamming the door behind her.

Dejected, Fresney slumped in his chair, holding his head in his hands.

# CHAPTER FOUR

Megan arrived at the hospital well in advance of her meeting with Kinkaid. On her way into the building, she bumped into Kacie Brendt, a fellow hospitalist who had been working at WGH for quite a while and with whom she had quickly developed a close friendship.

"Got a few to get a cup of joe to start the day?" asked Megan.

"Sure. My rounds don't begin for a little bit, so that's cool."

Once in the cafeteria, they each grabbed a coffee and sat at a small table near the window. Megan immediately checked her watch before taking a sip of her coffee.

Kacie took note and asked, "What's up?"

"On my way to a meeting with Art Kinkaid, and don't wanna be late. It seems he likes to meet with new staff after they've been here a bit."

"Yeah, he did the same with me when I was new."

"How long has he been the medical director here?"

"Let's see. I came on board two years ago, and he had just been appointed medical director."

"Was he already a physician on staff before assuming the position?"

"Uh-uh. He came from another hospital, but I don't know where. He's pretty tight-lipped about his background."

"Hmm. So, what's this meeting like?"

"Unless he's changed his routine, it's just a check-in with new hires for any problems. A pretty harmless discussion."

Megan nodded. "Actually, I think it's quite smart of him. Getting to know his new physicians to ensure all is copacetic. And I would think he identifies any issues needing attention in the process."

Kacie shrugged. "Well, at least he shows an interest in his physician staff. I've worked some places where they just throw you out on the wards and don't bother with you unless some disaster happens."

"Uh, don't you think that's a bit of an exaggeration, Kacie?"

"Yeah, I guess. But you know what I mean. It's nice to know someone's looking out for you and has your back. Hey, are you meeting in his office?"

"Mm-hmm."

"Cool. It's in the executive suite. I'm off in the same direction, so I'll walk over with you."

As they entered the suite, they overheard the tail end of the exchange between Sentini and Fresney and almost got knocked over by the board chair as she stormed out of the CEO's office, not seeming to notice either one of them.

"What the hell?" said Megan. "Do you know who she is?"

Kacie grinned. "Oh yeah. Elsbeth Sentini, chairperson of the hospital's board of directors."

"What's her story? She seemed kinda upset."

"Just a little, ya think? She's a high-powered attorney, and from what I've heard, a real power broker in town. And politically connected to boot. It appears this board thing is a diversion for her, although she seems to take it quite seriously. I hear she single-handedly managed to raise a ton of cash to support the hospital from local, and some not so local, donors." Kacie hesitated briefly. "And you didn't hear it from me, but the word is she feels entitled to a strong say in how this place runs."

Just then, Penny Salicio, the office assistant, called over to them. "Dr. McLoren? Dr. Kinkaid is ready for you."

"I guess that's your cue, Meg. I've gotta run anyway. Catch you later."

"Sure, Kace." And Megan followed Penny into the medical director's office.

# CHAPTER FIVE

Art Kinkaid was standing behind the desk when Megan entered his office. He appeared taller than she remembered from her initial interview with him.

He walked around the desk and nodded in the direction of a pair of comfortable armchairs facing each other on the other side of the room. "Let's sit over there. A little less formal than talking across my desk." He sat in one and waved his hand over to the other, inviting her to sit. "Something to drink? Coffee maybe?"

Megan smiled. "No thanks. I think I'm caffeinated enough for today."

"Yeah, I know what you mean. " He paused. "So, how have you found it here in Wallberg? I would imagine it's a good bit different from D.C."

Megan shifted in her chair. "I'd say it's a bit quieter here, yes, but also a whole lot less congested. I kind of like the change."

"Well, if you ever get a craving for the congestion you left behind, there's always Boston, a short drive down the road."

They both laughed.

Kinkaid folded his arms across his chest. "Any problems getting housing?"

"Not at all. The HR department was quite helpful, and I found a comfortable apartment not too far away, only a short drive."

"Good to hear. So, how's it going workwise? Any problems on the wards?"

"Not in the least. I have to say the nursing staff is great. They've really been patient while I learn the lay of the land, especially with the EMR. Same for the physicians." "I've always thought it's a shame all hospitals can't adopt the same electronic medical record system so providers wouldn't have to retrain on different systems if they move around."

"I happen to agree, Megan. Any other observations?"

She hesitated, uncertain whether or not to ask the question on her mind. "Well, there is something I have been wondering about."

"Really? Fire away."

"Maybe it's just my imagination, but it seems many of the legacy physicians here are a little disgruntled. I was wondering if there's something to that, if you don't mind me asking."

"Nonsense, of course I don't mind. And if I can say so myself, it's quite perceptive on your part."

He shifted in his chair and crossed his legs. "Let's see if I can provide some insight for you without getting too detailed. Most of the physicians you're referring to were in private practice before they joined the hospital staff. Their referrals to the hospital for advanced procedures were actually extremely important to the growth of WGH and its service to the community. Unfortunately, over time the landscape for physicians in small private practices changed. The EMR situation you just referenced was one of the stressors for them. In many cases, the cost of implementing an office-friendly system became prohibitive. And more importantly, the reimbursement environment began to worsen for them as well. Practice expenses were increasing while payor reimbursement for medical services decreased. Eventually, running a full-time office practice became financially untenable, while their capacity to see patients decreased as the complexity of running the practice increased."

Megan was certain she knew where he was going with this. "So, they came to the hospital for financial support?"

"Uh-huh. Except it became a legal issue, since it could be construed as hospital payments to physicians in return for patient referrals to the hospital for advanced services. A quid pro quo, if you will. So, management worked out an arrangement whereby the hospital purchased their practices and made them employees."

"What happened to their offices?"

"Good question. We offered to put a physician office building on the hospital campus, but with few exceptions, all wanted to stay in their current geographic location to accommodate their patients. So, we acquired their offices for a reasonable compensation based on various factors, and we cover all the office expenses. They're still able to admit and follow their patients in the hospital as medical needs dictate, or have a hospitalist such as yourself, care for the patient, who then returns to their physician's office after discharge. That was a very attractive arrangement for them, as many lived in close proximity to their offices and their patients did as well. We still went ahead with an office building on campus for new physicians who preferred to have an office closer to the hospital.

"That's not unique to this facility," said Megan. "It's sort of becoming a healthcare trend throughout the country for the same reasons."

"True. However, the security of a guaranteed salary and the financial benefit of not having to cover office expenses became overshadowed by the necessary loss of their control over practice operations. And if that wasn't bad enough, their need to meet required productivity measures for the hospital to afford this insanely expensive solution became a real sore spot for many of them. Much less so for the younger docs who never worked in a private practice environment anyway. Like you, for example. Sure, you're only here for twelve months before you leave for your fellowship. But for your generational colleagues who remain in primary care or hospitalist care, working for the hospital is all they've ever known, and there hasn't been the same radical change."

Megan nodded. "So, now these physicians have become disenchanted with forsaking their private practices for hospital employment, right?"

"You got it. Unfortunately, however, returning to their prior situation is not financially feasible for most, if not all of them. In reality, they really are better off and more secure in their current situation. And I think they all know it. But giving up autonomy is never easy, especially for highly trained professionals like physicians. Nevertheless, they could never afford to go back. Expenses are too high and reimbursement is going down, not up, especially by government payors."

Megan shook her head slowly. "Now I understand where they're coming from."

"To be honest, you'll likely be in a similar situation when you complete your fellowship, particularly in a specialized field like infectious disease. Hospital employment will undoubtedly be a no-brainer. Even more so if you continue your interest in research." He paused. "Is that still on your radar?

"At this point, yes."

"Hmm. Research is not very compatible with private practice."

Megan didn't respond, and Kinkaid broke the brief silence. "So, I'm sure those are the vibes you're getting. Any other concerns?

Megan started to stand. "No, I can't think of any."

He joined her and escorted her to the door. "Before you leave, I'd be remiss if I didn't share with you the incredibly positive feedback I've received from staff, both nurses and physicians, about you. And apparently patients adore you as well."

Megan beamed. "Thanks for mentioning it. And also, for the honest explanation and insight regarding the physician staff." Agreeing to his request that she bring any future concerns to his attention, she left the office to round on her patients. After leaving, she made a mental note of how engaging and supportive the medical director presented himself—and how thankful she was the board chair was no longer around to create another scene like she had witnessed earlier.

# CHAPTER SIX

When she returned to her office, Elsbeth Sentini was immediately approached by her assistant.

"Mr. Fresney from the hospital just called," said Gabby Wallum. "When I told him you hadn't arrived yet, he asked that you call him back as soon as you do."

"He did, huh?" Sentini grabbed a cup of coffee, proceeded to her office and sat at her desk.

Wallum followed and sat across from her. "Mm-hmm. Said it was important."

Sentini took a long sip of coffee. "Well then, you'll just have to let him know I'm with clients all day and we can talk at the upcoming board meeting."

Her assistant hesitated briefly before standing. "Okay, will do." She handed her boss several phone messages, then stood and left the room.

Sentini leaned back in her chair, rifled through the messages, then proceeded to make a call on her cell to someone who wasn't on the list.

The area code on the screen indicated the number was out of Boston, but the phone rang in Washington.

# CHAPTER SEVEN

"This meeting of the board of directors is now called to order," proclaimed Elsbeth Sentini, interrupting the typical pre-meeting chatter. It was five days after her outburst with Fresney about the financial report he had submitted. Since then, all she thought about was how she would deal with it at the full board meeting. Now it was showtime.

"Assuming all have read the most recent hospital financial report, it will be the main topic for today's discussion. I think we can all agree this report paints a very bleak outlook for the future of WGH." She tossed a fleeting glance over at Fresney. "Accordingly, I've asked Alan to work with Lyle Probey, our CFO, to prepare a proposal to reverse this downward trend in the hospital's finances."

She turned to Probey. "Lyle, please proceed with the details of your plan."

The CFO was short and balding, with ever-present, horned-rim glasses and perennially wrinkled suits. Today was no exception. Until now, he'd been slumped in his chair as if to make himself inconspicuous while Sentini was speaking. Now he sat up straight, cleared his throat and began providing a litany of rising operational costs contributing to the hospital's poor financial performance which, if continued, would foreshadow the hospital's failure. These ranged from such expenses as physician and other staff salaries, to rising cost of materials, medications and equipment maintenance. Added to the bleak situation with expenses was the stagnant, and in some cases, decreasing, government and private insurer payments adequate to offset such rising costs. He paused briefly, shuffled some papers and then went on to present a proposal to dramatically reduce these expenses as well as other discretionary spending.

When he finished speaking, a silence hung over the room like a pall until Sentini spoke. "I don't think I need to remind everyone here of the importance of this hospital to our community. Unfortunately, such extreme actions to reduce expenses as presented by Mr. Probey are not the answer to our financial crisis. On the contrary, it just represents the death knell of a failing institution."

Several board members demurely made eye contact with each other, but none spoke up.

"Cost cutting alone will not only hamper our ability to provide needed services," continued Sentini in a raised voice, "it will also have a devastating effect on staff morale."

She went silent briefly, letting her words resonate with the group. Several members nodded in agreement, but again, no one uttered a word.

"I have an alternate proposal," said Sentini. "One I believe makes much more sense, and should allow our hospital to instead grow and prosper even further." She hesitated, scanning the faces of everyone around the large table to confirm she held the attention of the entire group before continuing.

"I would like to propose we consider the services of an organization that has been successful in helping other hospitals extricate themselves from similar financial crises—Regnant Health Solutions."

Up to this point, Fresney had remained silent and stone-faced. Now he scowled and lashed out. "We're not going to be swallowed up by some damn hospital chain, so—"

"I'm not proposing such an arrangement, Alan," interrupted Sentini. "Are you even the least bit familiar with Oskar Wernuk and his company?"

She paused for effect before continuing, staring at Fresney, but he just frowned and remained silent. "Wernuk is not in the business of acquiring or merging hospitals. Instead, he founded his company for the specific purpose of helping healthcare organizations improve operations, revenue and expenses. In short, to become more efficient and financially stable."

Sentini leaned over her briefcase and retrieved enough informational packets for everyone present, and passed them around the table. "Take a few minutes to review Wernuk's bio, including how he came to form Regnant after a successful career in pharmacology sales and subsequently as a hospital chief operating officer. Then review the case studies of hospitals similar to ours that he and his team were able to turn around from failing to fiscally strong healthcare assets in their respective communities."

Everyone began intently reviewing their respective packet's contents while Sentini stepped out of the room briefly. She returned after about twenty minutes and called the meeting back to order. "I would like to introduce a motion we engage Regnant Health Solutions to perform an exploratory review of our organization, and present a proposal of engagement for their services if Wernuk and his team feel they can help us." She paused to make eye contact with everyone around the table except Fresney, who didn't look up.

"All in favor, please say aye."

The vote was unanimous in support of the proposal—with one exception. Fresney just glared at Sentini with no response as she spoke.

"Please let the record show the motion passed with unanimous support . . . except for one abstention. This meeting is now adjourned." Sentini grabbed her briefcase, stood up, and exited the room, walking down the hallway toward the door to the executive parking lot. Sitting in her car, she used her cell to select two numbers and send a two-word text to each: *We're on.*

# CHAPTER EIGHT

Dr. Allisyn McLoren sighed and collapsed into the chair at her office desk. She was exhausted after her most recent testimony with the Senate subcommittee that provided congressional oversight for her position as secretary of HHS, the Department of Health & Human Services.

As she looked around the room, she had an uncomfortable tightness in the pit of her stomach. Even though the office had been totally renovated since the dismissal and subsequent indictment of her predecessor for fraud, it still reminded her of the numerous strained interactions that took place between herself and her supervisor in this very same room when Allisyn was FDA commissioner.

Her musings were interrupted by her former assistant at the FDA whom Allisyn had insisted on joining her at HHS.

"Senator Courte would like to speak with you," said Ginger.

Wendell Courte was the senior senator from Massachusetts and a member of the committee that oversaw HHS. He wasn't particularly a fan of Allisyn, always taking an opposing position of hers on healthcare legislation.

And although she wouldn't admit it to anyone—except maybe Ginger—the sentiment was mutual.

She sighed. "Okay, you can put his call through."

"Uh, he's actually waiting right outside the door."

"He's here?"

Ginger gave her a sheepish look and shrugged.

Allisyn pushed her chair back from her desk. "Damn!"

"Should I tell him you're on the phone or otherwise busy with something?"

"No, don't bother. He'd probably say he'd wait anyway. Go ahead and let him in."

Ginger left the room, but only a few seconds later reopened the door to admit the senator.

As he entered, Allisyn began to stand.

He held up his hand in a "stop" gesture, then pulled a chair up to the desk facing her and sat down. "Please stay seated, Madam Secretary," he said. "This won't take long."

Allisyn leaned back in her chair, suppressing a gagging sensation at his gratuitous introduction before she spoke. "Go ahead, then."

Courte leaned forward, placing his arms on the desk and assuming an aggressive posture. "When you were discussing healthcare financing at today's hearing, it seems your focus is on controlling hospital and physician charges. I believe more emphasis should be placed on the insurance industry. They underpay for services while their executives get fat with exorbitant salaries and bonuses garnered from escalating patient premiums. In the meantime, hospitals and physicians are shortchanged with stagnant or reduced reimbursement."

Allisyn leaned back, elbows on the arms of her chair. "So, what would you propose?"

"Me? I think it's within your purview to explore and propose ideas to rectify the situation."

She steepled her fingers. "I see, senator. Unfortunately, I don't think you and I can resolve this issue today, and certainly not by ourselves. Let's say I investigate this further and see if we can have a more substantial discussion going forward and include the necessary stakeholders." "Just one thing, though." She continued. "HHS may have its hands tied to some extent in dictating reimbursement levels to private insurers."

Courte continued to stare at her, but didn't respond immediately. She was about to stand and walk him to the door when he finally spoke.

"I guess it's a start," he said. "And while you're at it, please address the issue of withholding reimbursement to physicians and hospitals for new medical technologies, testing, and services."

Suspecting he was going to drag this on, Allisyn was determined to thwart further discussion. She stood and began walking toward the door. "If you have nothing further to discuss, senator, I have some important phone calls to make. I'll let you know when I have some additional insight into your concerns."

"I look forward to it, and thank you for your consideration."

Allisyn opened the door and addressed Ginger. "Please see Senator Courte out."

After he exited, she returned to her desk, sat down and began musing about where his conversation was really going. Although she couldn't put her finger on it, the thought there was something more to what he said continued to nag at her for the remainder of the day.

# CHAPTER NINE

Megan had just finished her morning rounds and was headed to the cafeteria for a quick bite before an afternoon conference when her cell pinged. She pulled it out of her jacket pocket and saw it was from the executive office assistant, Penny Salicio. *Please come to the office as soon as possible.*

Even though she was starving, the urgency of the cryptic message begged immediacy. So, she decided to go see what it was about, and grab a sandwich afterward on the way to the conference.

When Megan arrived at the executive suite, Salicio was on the phone, just listening and apparently taking some notes. When she caught Megan's eye, she pointed to a chair and held up one finger, soundlessly mouthing "one minute." Sure enough, in short order she was off the phone and looked up at Megan. "Thanks for coming so quickly."

Megan looked at her with a furrowed brow. "No problem. What's up?"

"Do you know a Detective Conyers? From Baltimore?"

Megan stiffened in her chair, eyes wide. "Uh-huh, I do. What about him?"

"He called here trying to reach you. Said he didn't have your cell number, but heard from someone you were working here."

"What did he want?"

"Didn't say. Just asked if you could call him as soon as possible. Here's his number." She handed Megan a piece of paper.

Megan took the paper and just sat there, staring down at it with a slight hand tremor and quickening breath.

"Are you okay?" said Salicio.

Megan looked up. "Wha… what?"

"Okay. Are you okay? You look a little pale. Do you want some water?"

Megan shook her head. "No…I mean yeah, I'm fine."

"Water?"

"Sure. Water would be great. Thanks." She reached for the cup Penny brought her, took a small sip, and slumped back in her chair.

Penny gently put a hand on her shoulder. "Feeling better?"

"Uh-huh. It's just some old memories." She took another drink, this time a healthy gulp. "I guess I need to call him."

"Why don't you use the small conference room here? That way you can have some privacy, and I'll be around in case you need something."

Megan hesitated, looking a little confused. "Uh, yeah. That would be great. Thanks."

After satisfying herself Megan was okay, Penny left her sitting at the conference room table and closed the door.

Megan took out her phone and dialed. Her anxiety was slowly dissipating.

The call was answered after two rings. "Hello?"

"Detective Conyers?"

"Yes."

"This is Megan. Megan McLoren, returning your call."

"Oh, thanks for getting back to me, Megan. Sorry, I didn't have your cell number and"

"You could have called Allisyn for it."

"Hmm. You're right. I didn't think of that."

"How did you know I worked here?"

He hesitated. "Paul Cortez told me."

"Paul? Agacia's husband?

"Yes. He told me you and her were close friends, and—"

"Yeah, we were in residency together and were pretty tight. Wait, why were you talking with Paul about me? What's going on?"

Megan thought she heard a deep sigh before he spoke.

"Well, that's just it, Megan. I'm sorry, but Agacia is dead."

"What? No way! I just spoke with her a few weeks ago. Why didn't Paul call me?"

"He's very distraught. Said he couldn't bear to talk right now. Asked me to speak with you."

She slumped back in her chair. "Was she sick?"

"No. She fell."

"Fell? Where? What happened?"

"She fell, out the window—of their fifth-floor apartment in South Baltimore."

"Are you serious? That's ridiculous."

"I'm afraid all signs point to suicide."

Megan almost dropped her phone. "Suicide? No way Agacia would take her own life! It must have been an accident."

"Possibly, yes. And to be fair, we're still investigating. But there's a witness. It was late at night. He was walking home from work and saw her in the window. It was dark and he can't be a hundred percent sure, but he said she was poised on the windowsill for a brief period like she was hesitating, straddling it with one leg out, when it appeared she deliberately pulled her other leg over, and jumped.

Megan felt her throat tighten and pressure in her chest as she began to cry.

"I'm so sorry, Megan. Did she seem upset, or concerned about her job when you last spoke?"

"Not particularly." She sniffled and dabbed her eyes with the sleeve of her jacket. "I mean, she was a little frustrated with her workload, but she really liked the hospital and quickly made some friends. She grew up in Baltimore, and felt fortunate to get her first job at a hospital in a community halfway between the city and Washington, and yet still live in Baltimore.

"That's it? Nothing else? Paul said some work-related issues seemed to be bothering her."

"Yeah, she mentioned having a little problem adjusting to the hospital's routines. Like anything else, there's variation from one hospital to another. And the EMR, the electronic medical record, was a little challenging. But learning a new system is not unusual either. And apparently there were some glitches with patient billing and chart entries, although she didn't go into any detail. She was a little frustrated because administration simply dismissed it as a minor issue and reassured her it was being addressed. I can't imagine it would cause her to do anything like this, though. She certainly didn't hint at it. " She paused. "What did Paul say?" "Pretty much the same. Except he described her as more than frustrated—a little angry, actually—at administration for dismissing her concerns about a number of patient billing complaints.

"Hmm. She didn't go into any such details when we spoke. But sounds like typical hospital administrator speak. "Stick to patient care and stay out of administrative issues."

"Yeah, that's what Paul said. Although he thought her frustration was increasing. I guess she couldn't get it out of her head and it took its toll emotionally." He paused. "I'm aware physicians have a relatively high rate of suicide. An unfortunate outcome from all the stress of the job, I presume. Must be what happened with her."

"I . . . guess. Except Agacia always had it together. She never really let such things get to her. Where was Paul when she…when it happened?

"He was out of town, on business. He's pretty broken up."

"No kidding. They were an ideal couple. Really cared for each other. I'll give him a call."

"If you think of anything else, Megan, please call me. Anything at all."

"Will do, Detective."

"Hal, It's Hal. Remember? That's what we agreed on."

"Yeah, yeah. I remember. By the way, how's the shoulder?"

"Good as new. Pretty lucky, I guess. You take care. I'll let you know if we find out anything else."

"Thanks, Hal."

She disconnected and put her head down in her hands, elbows on the table, eyes still moist. After about five minutes, she got up and left for her conference, thanking Penny, and wiping away her tears. She bypassed the cafeteria without a thought of stopping. She no longer had an appetite.

# CHAPTER TEN

"Thank you all for attending this important follow-up meeting so soon after our last one."

Elsbeth Sentini had called the WGH board members back together to hear Oskar Wernuk's assessment and recommendations regarding whether his company, Regnant Health Solutions, would be able to help the hospital avoid what appeared to be a pending financial collapse.

Wernuk was seated across the table from Sentini and placed his hand on the shoulder of a man sitting next to him. "Before I get started, I'd like to introduce Ty Prendersen, here. He's our operational director and oversees any project we undertake."

Tight-lipped, Prendersen simply nodded in acknowledgement.

Wernuk removed a large stack of binders, each about one inch thick with documents, and passed them around to the board members.

"Each folder," he said, "contains detailed findings regarding the financial issues facing you here at Wallberg General, our recommendations for averting further deterioration of your situation, and equally important, reversing the trend going forward. I will leave it to each of you to review the details. For today, I, along with Ty, will summarize our position." He looked to Sentini. "Acceptable, Madam Chairperson?"

She looked to CEO Fresney sitting next to her. "Alan? Agree?"

Expressionless, he simply nodded.

She turned to Wernuk. "Great. Please proceed."

Wernuk then presented a litany of operational inefficiencies, along with recommendations for correction or improvement, including updating the hospital's electronic medical record system, as well as its financial and billing software, to Regnant Health's proprietary systems. He followed with a number of missed marketing opportunities for the hospital's elective services, and a brief outline of how his team would engage the hospital in a successful marketing campaign to increase visibility in the community.

When the duo finished, Sentini looked around and mostly saw expressions registering agreement with what the group just heard.

Then she addressed Wernuk and Prendersen: "I want to thank you both for this enlightening presentation. The board will discuss your recommendations and vote on whether to proceed with engaging your services. I'll contact you with our decision."

Wernuk thanked the group for their attention, then together with Prendersen left the meeting.

A brief discussion ensued, followed by a vote. This time it was unanimous in favor of the motion to proceed, with no abstentions or nays. Fresney had reluctantly deferred to the will of the board.

Sentini ended the meeting by formally proclaiming the result. "Let the record show the proposal to engage Oskar Wernuk and his team in an exploratory review of the hospital's financial and operational functions has passed by unanimous vote, and the process is officially approved going forward. Therefore, this meeting is adjourned."

Everyone in the room sported a look of satisfaction and offered positive comments on the outcome of the proposal as they prepared to leave, with one exception—Alan Fresney, who remained silent, his face seemingly frozen in a disapproving scowl.

# CHAPTER ELEVEN

Megan was startled awake by the vibration of the plane as it landed. Looking at her watch, she wasn't surprised she'd slept the entire flight from Boston's Logan Airport to BWI—Baltimore-Washington International. She was exhausted from work, and the awful news of her best friend's horrible death was overwhelming. Besides, the ungodly early hour of her flight hadn't helped. Sleep was a needed respite before attending services for Agacia Cortez.

After disembarking, she got a rental car and headed north on 95. Following the navigation directions from her cell, she arrived at the south Baltimore funeral home forty-five minutes later.

Megan parked a short walk from the venue and paused before entering. She took a deep breath, hoping it would clear the heavy feeling in her chest. Unfortunately, it didn't have the desired effect, and she was already fighting back tears. She entered the building and went directly to the room where the services were being held. Although it appeared full to capacity, there were only a handful of familiar faces. She immediately noticed the absence of a casket. Instead, an urn had been placed atop a table next to a framed photo of Agacia.

As she scanned the full room, she caught sight of Paul Cortez and made her way over to him. The redness of his eyes and pained look on his face as their gazes met broke her heart, and tears trickled down her cheeks.

He immediately approached her and they hugged in an embrace of mutual sorrow.

"I'm sorry, Paul, so sorry," she choked out, barely intelligibly.

Without saying anything, he hugged her tighter for a few moments, took her by the hand to another room that was empty and quiet, then sat in chairs facing each other.

"I don't understand, Paul. Why would Agacia do such a thing? Why?"

His lips slightly parted, he shook his head slowly. "I don't know, Megan. I just don't know."

"Could it have been an accident?"

He sighed heavily. "You knew her just as well I did, Megan. She was always so cautious and careful. I don't see how. Besides, the detective, uh…"

"Conyers, Hal Conyers."

"Right, Conyers. He said the description from the eyewitness below indicated she made deliberate motions indicating intent."

"Did the police find a suicide note?"

"No. They scoured the apartment but nothing turned up. And I couldn't find anything when I went through her personal notes and belongings."

"Hmm. Do you have any idea why she would take her own life?"

Looking down at his folded hands, he shrugged and shook his head. Uh-uh."

"Not to pry, but was all okay between the two of you?"

Paul looked up at her. "Of course. We had even begun discussing starting a family."

Megan pursed her lips and slowly shook her head. She knew how important this was to Agacia.

"Paul, Detective Conyers said you mentioned some—how should I say this—some issues she was dealing with at the hospital. Could you elaborate a little?"

"The hospital had just replaced their entire computer system with new software, and apparently there were some glitches."

"Glitches? Like what?"

"She didn't go into detail, but it seems there were some irregularities with the new electronic medical record system they had recently installed. I didn't really understand it, and she didn't elaborate further. Anyway, she started checking around, and other staff were experiencing the same frustrations with the EMR. When she brought it to the attention of a hospital administrator, he indicated it was all related to the system conversion, was being checked out, and would be corrected."

"Hmm. Anything else?"

"Yeah. The administrator told her not to get involved, insisting administration was aware of the problem and was working with the vendor to correct it. But what really had her miffed was the way they ignored her concerns and told her to back off, just care for the patients and stop looking for more problems with the system. She felt they were also dismissing patient complaints about billing. After that encounter, she started brooding about it and seemed almost obsessed, even though I told her to let it go."

"She mentioned the same to me when we last spoke, but I didn't get the impression she was that upset."

"Upset?" Paul became more animated. "It was more like angry. I figured it was just... uh, what do you call it? Physician burnout?"

"Yeah, except it's been suggested the term "moral injury" is more appropriate."

"Huh?"

"It's well accepted physicians have found their work more and more challenging, with greater complexities and growing patient loads. In other words, the need to accomplish the impossible task of satisfying the patient, hospital, insurer, and the physician herself. In the context of healthcare, instead of the term 'burnout,' which implies the problem lies within the physician, "moral injury" more accurately locates the source of the distress external to the physician and instead within the business framework of healthcare itself."

Paul's tone softened. "Sorta makes sense. At least I can appreciate such a conflict for Agacia. She always felt more concern for the patient than the system." "I know. It's what made her such a great doctor. Anyway, frustration can lead to despondency and depression, which together can be followed by suicidal thoughts. And the incidence of suicide is indeed known to be higher among physicians than other professions."

"Does that mean you're agreeing with the detective? Acacia committed suicide?"

"I can't really say, Paul, but since the eyewitness description of her seems to indicate intentional rather than accidental, and in view of what Agacia was dealing with at work, I sure think the concept of moral injury leading to a feeling of helplessness and depression is consistent with what she was struggling with."

There was a brief, uncomfortable silence between them before Paul spoke. "Well, I guess now I have some understanding of the conflict she was dealing with and led to her … to such a terrible action. I only wish I could have helped with her struggles. If I only knew."

"Yes, if you only knew. Except, of course you had no way of knowing. Because it was Agacia's nature—true to her moral compass—and at the same time private with her feelings. She felt this was her struggle, not yours, and no need to bother you with it."

Eyes closed, he accepted her heartfelt embrace once again before they walked together back into the reception room and she left to catch her return flight to Boston.

# CHAPTER TWELVE

Ty Prendersen, Regnant's operational director who would be overseeing the company's project with WGH, had just completed the first of several presentations regarding the specifics of the transformation he would be leading for the hospital. Every employee was required to attend one of these informational sessions, followed by operational training specific to their individual role at the hospital.

He explained how this engagement was designed to enhance operational performance and improve productivity, with the goal of augmenting and stabilizing the hospital's financial status without random cost cutting. This, he emphasized, would make the organization more attractive to lenders in providing the financing required to expand healthcare services to the community while maintaining, and likely improving, the current level of clinical care provided to patients.

By the time he finished providing some of the specifics, most everyone in the audience was calmly nodding their heads, signaling apparent approval of the plan.

One attendee wasn't so enthused. Kacie Brendt's concern related to the implementation of an entirely new EMR— Electronic Medical Record— especially since it was central to the care of patients. And this one would be proprietary to Regnant. She had been through this kind of transition previously at another hospital. Smooth and uncomplicated were not words she would use to describe the process.

She filed out of the room with everyone else, not looking forward to what might lie ahead.

# CHAPTER THIRTEEN

Megan and Kacie each quietly sipped their beer at the Campus Pub, a local watering hole often frequented by hospital staff when off duty.

When Megan returned from her trip to Baltimore, she caught up on her patients, who had been covered by her fellow hospitalists in her absence. As it happened, both her and Kacie's shifts for the week ended before the coming weekend started, and they decided to share a little down time together.

Megan had just finished telling her about Agacia Cortez's tragic death by suicide.

Kacie was appropriately sympathetic but refrained from probing for details. Instead, she shifted the conversation to the Regnant Health training session they had both attended.

"So, what do you think, Megan? Will this entire program change anything here?"

Megan was gazing off to the side, lost in thought.

"Megan?"

"Huh? Did you say something?"

"Mm-hmm. About this Regnant company and their program." Kacie paused before changing the subject. "You need to move on, Meg. I know it's tough and I appreciate how important your friendship with Agacia was, but you need to move on."

"Yeah, I know. It's just that . . . I mean, I still can't believe she would do such a thing, or even understand why if she did. Megan paused. "I'm sorry, Kace. What was that about Regnant?"

Kacie flashed a gentle smile. "Do you think all this change is going to make anything better? Or will it only be an exercise in futility, and the hospital will continue its financial downward spiral. It certainly wouldn't be the first hospital of its size to struggle financially in today's healthcare environment."

"Sure," said Megan "But it does make some sense. After all, efficiency, maximizing productivity, and eliminating waste can have a positive effect, not only on financial performance, but on quality outcomes and safety as well."

Kacie took a long swig of her beer, finishing off what was left. "Let's just hope you're right and all this change results in the desired improvement effect for the hospital, especially the new EMR. And on that note, I need to get some rest before my next shift. You?"

Megan nodded. "Same. I'm worn out—physically and emotionally."

Both standing, Megan gently held Kacie by the shoulders and gave her a friendly hug. "Thanks for listening, Kace. I guess it makes you my new BFF."

They both laughed, and went their separate ways to get some much-needed rest.

# CHAPTER FOURTEEN

After a weekend of doing nothing, Megan returned to work the following Monday, well-rested in spite of her inability to take her mind off Agacia's demise.

She passed by the Medical Staff office and picked up a list of her patients to see if she had any new admissions she needed to attend to before rounding on her current complement of patients in house. Attached to the list was a note from Penny Salicio requesting her to call the office. Apparently, Art Kinkaid wanted her to stop by when she had a chance. Not knowing what the issue was or its level of urgency, she immediately called Salicio and set a time for later in the afternoon.

---

Kinkaid was leaning over Salicio's desk, engaged in a conversation with her when Megan arrived in the office suite. He looked up and abruptly turned away from his assistant. "Thanks for stopping by, Megan. Come on into my office."

She followed him in and took a seat, a little tense and anxious about the nature of this meeting so soon after their previous encounter. "Is there something wrong, AR—uh, Dr. Kinkaid?"

"Not at all, Megan." He proffered a half-smile. "And Art is fine."

She relaxed her shoulders and nodded, acknowledging his directive.

"Penny shared with me the unfortunate news you recently received about your friend, and I just wanted to extend my sincere condolences." . . . "Not to pry, but do you know what happened?"

Megan hesitated briefly, before providing an abbreviated version of what she knew, refraining from the details of Agacia's supposed contentious interaction with hospital administration. "I just can't believe she would take her own life, as they suspect."

"Hmm. I can understand how upsetting this must be for you, Megan. Does she have family?"

"Her husband, Paul."

"Would you like to have a little extra time off to get through this? We can certainly have your patients covered and—"

"No! I need to get back to work. I'll miss her, sure. But I need to move on."

"Of course. ... Still, if you ever need to talk it out, we do have counseling services."

"Thanks. I'll keep that in mind"

"Have you gotten out much since coming here? You know, socially?"

"Not much, really."

"I'll tell you what. Why don't I introduce you to some good restaurants? We have a number in town. Italian, Mexican, steakhouses. You choose, and you can be my guest."

Megan hesitated, not wanting any entanglements. *Now what do I do? I guess a simple dinner can't hurt. I can handle that, and maybe get my mind cleared out.*

"Pesto," she said.

"Huh?"

"Pesto. As in pasta al pesto."

"Ahh. Now I get it. Italian."

She smiled. "My favorite."

"Okay," he said as he stood up. "We'll agree on an evening and I'll take care of the restaurant. Deal?"

"Uh, sure." She stood and walked toward the door, hesitated, then looked back at him. "Thanks for your understanding about Agacia."

He only nodded without saying a word.

She walked out, a queasy feeling in her stomach. She knew this was a totally different situation, but still couldn't rid her mind of thoughts about the last time she was alone with a man.

# CHAPTER FIFTEEN

"Pretty impressive," said Elsbeth Sentini. Some time had passed since the engagement with Regnant Health Solutions began, and she was meeting with Alan Fresney, Art Kinkaid, Oskar Wernuk, Ty Prendersen and CFO Lyle Probey to review the hospital's latest financial reports. Sentini's response reflected the significant improvement accrued since partnering with Regnant, Wernuk's hospital management company.

Everyone was anticipating the report except Fresney, who remained skeptical.

"Ty's done an excellent job," said Wernuk, "implementing the operational changes that have increased productivity and decreased waste while maintaining WGH's high standard of patient care." He turned to Kinkaid. "Would you agree, Doctor? About the standard of care?"

Kinkaid nodded. "Uh-huh. The clinical staff were a little hesitant at first, but they've come around to the operational changes, and for the most part feel their clinical environment has improved as well."

"And they've all adapted to our new EMR?" asked Wernuk.

Kinkaid leaned forward, folding his hands on the table. "It seems so, yes. Of course, learning a new clinical system produces some anxiety in the beginning. Overall, however, this transition has gone smoothly, and the new system appears well accepted at present. Although I can't speak to the non-clinical aspects of the EMR, like finances. "I can comment on that," said Probey enthusiastically. "I must admit, I was skeptical at first. But it's proven to be a big improvement from our legacy system. Our payors have been responding well, and our revenue cycle has improved remarkably."

Conspicuously, Fresney was not asked to provide his impression of the transition.

"In summary, then," said Sentini, "it looks like we're moving along nicely." She turned to Wernuk.

"Oskar, would you like to explain what you and I discussed?"

Wernuk sat upright and leaned forward while making stern eye contact with each of them individually. "I do have one observation to act on. The hospital has a very well-equipped cardiac catheterization laboratory, that unfortunately is not being used. I discussed this with Ms. Sentini, who confirmed your interventional cardiac program has been defunct for some time. I don't know, nor is it necessary for me to know, why. What I can say, however, is in surveying your community and healthcare market, cardiology and its interventional offshoot represent a great opportunity for this hospital." He nodded over at Sentini. "I've discussed this with Elsbeth, and we agree this should be rectified."

"What?" blurted out Fresney in a raised voice. "This is news to me." He shot daggers at Sentini. "Why wasn't I part of the discussion?"

"Easy, Alan, Easy. It was just an informal discussion Oskar and I had. Of course, we were going to speak with you about it. And now that it's on the table, I think we should seriously consider reviving the interventional cardiac program. All that expensive equipment is sitting unused while a need for the service in the community goes unmet."

"Hold on," said Fresney. "Not so fast. It's going to take an awful lot to revive such a program. The equipment must be brought up to appropriate standards, and we'll have to meet all state requirements for the program, then survive a rigorous accreditation and regulatory process." He paused. "Not to mention recruiting a seasoned interventional cardiologist to set up the program and lead it clinically. If you ask me, it's quite a tall order, and a risky endeavor."

"I certainly understand the challenges here," said Sentini. "But I don't think we should just dismiss this out of hand, Alan." She looked over at Kinkaid. "You're the clinician here, Art. What do you think?"

Kinkaid glanced furtively at Fresney, then turned back to Sentini. "I think it's doable. The equipment is all top of the line, and although it's been dormant, it has very few hours of use. We should be able to get it up and running, no problem. And regulatory and state approval technically shouldn't be an issue, provided we have a top-notch interventional cardiologist to run the program, make sure all the requirements are met, and we can recruit seasoned support staff, like the requisite technicians."

"That's where I can help," said Wernuk. "We've done this before, and been quite successful in recruiting that kind of talent. I have no doubt we can do the same for you here."

"Great," said Sentini. "We'll have you prepare a proposal for how to move forward with such a project, including helping us recruit the appropriate staff, as well as the potential return on investment to the hospital. As for the regulatory and accreditation issues, I may be able to provide some assistance on that front. At a minimum, I think we should continue to look into it. Anyone disagree?"

Fresney shook his head. "I think we should go slowly on this. There are a lot of potential pitfalls that could be damaging to the hospital in the long run."

Sentini frowned. "That's what we have Oskar and his team for. No sense in being a naysayer until we have a solid roadmap to review." . . . "And with that said, I think we're done here for today."

They all rose and left the conference room —except Sentini. She took out her cell and called her office to speak with her assistant. "Arrange an urgent teleconference with all the board members for later today. We have an important decision to make."

# CHAPTER SIXTEEN

"Let's sit," said Elsbeth Sentini as she entered Alan Fresney's office and closed the door.

After her teleconference with the remainder of the board, she had arranged to meet with him the following day.

"I'm not going to beat around the bush and drag this out, Alan."

The blank expression on Fresney's face didn't betray what he might be thinking. "Get on with it, then."

Arms folded, Sentini leaned back in her chair across from him. "The board has decided to replace you as hospital CEO."

Fresney leaned forward, hands firmly on his desk in an aggressive posture. "Replace me? With whom?"

"I'll be assuming the position on an interim basis until we find a suitable replacement."

"You? Our overbearing board chair? Now that is rich! How did you get your loyal followers to agree to a coup this time? What did you promise them?"

"You can't seriously tell me you didn't see this coming, Alan, given the way you've resisted this engagement with Regnant from the very beginning. Not one among us believe you've bought into Wernuk's proposal and are committed to making it successful. And the board feels it must be successful for this hospital to survive. Quite frankly, your outburst at yesterday's meeting with Wernuk about the proposal for an interventional cardiology program, and your negative position regarding its implementation, was the final straw. The board met by phone conference last evening and unanimously voted to remove you from the position."

Fresney was speechless, his jaw clenched, eyebrows furrowed, and a deep reddish discoloration of his face extending down to his neck.

"You will, of course, receive a generous severance package. " Sentini paused. "There's no doubt, Alan, this organization must move forward, and Regnant seems to provide the roadmap to success."

Fresney scoffed. "And you really think there will be a magical turnaround here?"

Sentini pursed her lips and slowly shook her head. "That right there is the negative attitude the board just couldn't tolerate. Everyone was convinced you wouldn't cooperate with Wernuk's team, and that is unacceptable."

Fresney slouched in his chair. "I guess that's it, then. … Good luck with your grand plan for the hospital."

The sarcasm wasn't lost on Sentini. "We'll be letting the staff know very soon, so the quicker you wrap things up, the better." She stood, walked over to the door, then stopped and looked back. "I'll let your assistant know to process all the necessary paperwork for your smooth separation."

Then she left, while Fresney remained sitting at his desk, pondering the future of Wallberg General Hospital.

# CHAPTER SEVENTEEN

Partially covered by a bedsheet, Elsbeth Sentini rolled onto her side and propped up her arm, elbow on the bed and hand supporting her head.

"So how did your little meeting with the esteemed secretary go?"

Senator Wendell Courte was lying on his back, head on a pillow. "The HHS secretary? Unfortunately, the good doctor wasn't quite as receptive to my suggestion as I had hoped."

Sentini frowned. "Meaning?"

"Meaning she seems focused on controlling hospital and physician charges and less concerned about ensuring appropriate reimbursement by insurers and our own government payors, especially for new, state of the art tests and procedures."

"Hmm. That's a problem."

"Yeah, so I told her. She said we could put together a working group to study the issue."

"Right. Like that's gonna happen any time soon."

"Whatever. I'll keep the pressure on her."

Sentini shifted her hips, and when the sheet covering her shoulders slipped off and down onto the bed, she didn't bother pulling it back up. "That reminds me. One more thing. I need your help with a regulatory issue at the hospital. Has to do with reviving our defunct interventional cardiology program. We may require some assistance with getting accreditation approval from the state to move forward."

"No problem," he said, looking over at her without making eye contact, and instead focusing on her naked body. "Get me the details and I'll take care of it." He completely threw off his side of the sheets and started to sit up. "It's been nice, Elsbeth—as always—but I think I should be going."

She glanced over at him and smiled. "Really? I don't think so." And she scooted over next to him as he laid back down.

# CHAPTER EIGHTEEN

Dr. Trevor Quinne was joined by Elsbeth Sentini, Art Kinkaid and Oskar Wernuk in the hospital board room. Alan Fresney's conspicuous absence was ignored by all.

Quinne was an interventional cardiologist with an impressive resume who had been recruited by Wernuk and approved by the WGH team to restart the hospital's cardiac program. Unknown to all but Wernuk, Quinne had accomplished just that for several other hospitals as part of Regnant Health engagements.

The report was straightforward. The equipment had laid dormant, was upgraded, tested and in full operating order. All program and staffing requirements were put in place and approved by Kinkaid as hospital medical director.

Most importantly, WGH received full accreditation and regulatory approval from the appropriate state and local agencies to resume its interventional cardiology program in record time. The crucial role Senator Wendell Courte and his political connections played in making sure it took place was known only to Sentini.

Quinne would stay in place as program director and primary clinical provider. The program was slated to reopen with a media blitz alerting the public to procedures available and integration with the WGH emergency department to care for patients with acute cardiac conditions.

The last component of the program, at Wernuk's suggestion, was for the hospital's public relations department to arrange "heart fairs" throughout the WGH patient catchment area. The purpose was to provide low or no-cost screening of patients for mild or "sub-clinical" cardiac signs or symptoms, with referral to the hospital's center for the testing and possible treatment of so-called "silent cardiac disease."

The meeting ended with unanimous approval and consent to move forward with the program, and the group dispersed, satisfied with the plan.

# CHAPTER NINETEEN

Megan and Kacie were back at the Campus Pub for another late Friday afternoon unwinding session, featuring their mutually favorite form of liquid sustenance, after a busy week of caring for patients. They each held a mug of beer, with a half-full pitcher and a small bowl of barely touched pretzel bites between them.

After commiserating with each other about not having any social plans for the weekend, their talk reverted to work.

Kacie took a sip of beer, then leaned back in her chair. "Have you met the new cardiologist?"

Megan tilted her head down and looked up at Kacie. "I was at his introductory reception a few weeks back, but other than that I haven't spoken with him. Why?"

Kacie frowned. "Just asking. He seems to have gotten awfully busy, awfully fast. And the great majority of his patients, at least on my service, have been elective, non-acute catheterizations. Got me thinking where all those patients have come from."

"Good question." nodded Megan. Do you think those community heart fairs the hospital has been holding are generating referrals?"

Kacie frowned. "Who knows? but I wouldn't be surprised. A patient would only need the slightest hint of symptoms to suspect cardiac issues, and it's off to the cath lab for a nuclear stress test and a cardiac angiogram, with possible stent placement for prophylaxis."

Megan gave her a sideways glance. "Do you seriously believe that's what's happening?"

Kacie shrugged. "Dunno, but it wouldn't be the first time I've encountered a medical proceduralist blurring the lines between benign and clinically significant symptoms to justify an intervention."

"Wow! Your cynical view of your colleagues' professionalism is a little unnerving."

"I may be a little jaded, but what can I say? It happens. Tell me you can seriously say you've never witnessed it yourself, Megan."

Megan sighed and slowly shook her head in disbelief, but didn't respond, fearful she would offend Kacie with her opinion of what she thought of her friend's perspective.

Kacie finished off what was left in her beer mug and broke the silence. "Whatever. I'm sure administration is happy with the financial benefits of the program—and that keeps all of us employed."

Megan remained silent, thinking what a different side of Kacie she'd just witnessed for the first time. She drank what was left of her beer and was about to feign exhaustion as a reason for leaving early when Kacie spoke.

"Tell me, Megan. Have you had any patients complain about their charts in the EMR, or about bills for services?

"I can't say no, but I haven't been overwhelmed with such complaints. Why?"

"Just wondering if it's only me. I've had a good number of my patients complaining their healthcare insurer is questioning diagnoses submitted, and I've noticed some documentation discrepancies in the EMR, as well as some tests done that I didn't know about."

"Hmm. I assume the patients have asked you to justify necessity to the insurers, which is more paperwork and taking up time you don't have, right?" "Yeah, except in most of the cases, I didn't enter the diagnosis or order the test in question."

"Uh, no offense, Kace, but is it possible you actually did enter the diagnoses and order those tests? You know how hectic it can get in the clinic—busy with multiple patients, checking lab and x-ray results, phone calls for prescriptions, etcetera."

"No way!" said Kacie indignantly in a loud voice. "You think I'm that incompetent or absentminded?"

"No, of course not. I'm just saying, you know, with all the distractions in the clinic, we all get a little frazzled at times. Sorry, Kace." She waited for her friend to cool down. "Did you think of running it by this Prendersen guy? After all, he's the operations guru. Maybe he can figure out what's going on."

Kacie nodded. As a matter of fact, I did exactly that."

"And?"

"He said he checked the system and guess what?"

Megan leaned forward. "I have no idea, but it better be good."

Kacie scoffed. "He said the system actually did record me as the physician entering the diagnoses being questioned and ordering the tests."

"What? Must be some screw-up with the system."

Kacie chewed on her lower lip. "What do you expect from a non-clinician?"

"Speaking of which," said Megan, "I was going to suggest bringing this up with Art Kinkaid. Like you said before, it's good to have someone who looks out for you and has your back."

"Yeah, I guess. I didn't really think of talking with him about it, but seems like a good idea since you mention it."

Megan leaned back in her chair, looking satisfied. "Let me know what he says, okay?"

"Sure will, Meg. And keep an eye out yourself for this issue with your patients. You never know."

They finished off what remained of the beer and left in separate directions.

As she drove home, Megan was thinking how oddly familiar Kacie's story was.

# CHAPTER TWENTY

Dr. Mitchell—Mitch—Harwick stepped back and looked intently at the video monitor screen. As director of WGH's radiology department, one of his regular tasks was reviewing x-rays and procedure videos to ensure no abnormalities were missed and left unmentioned in the final report that had been issued. He especially focused on readouts where a serious abnormality had been identified and video recordings that involved invasive procedures.

At the moment, he was reviewing one of the first coronary angiograms performed in the newly renovated and operational interventional cardiology suite by the new cardiologist and director of the department, Dr. Trevor Quinne.

Procedures performed in the suite included x-ray visualization of the arteries of the heart using contrast—a special dye—to look for blockages or other abnormalities that could be the cause of cardiac conditions ranging from mild chest discomfort and/or shortness of breath, to more severe symptoms and potentially fatal heart attacks—myocardial infarction in medical speak. If such a narrowing of the arteries is identified radiologically by performing this catheterization and coronary angiogram, the blocked artery can be propped open from within by performing an angioplasty—the insertion of a balloon or a stent—sort of a metal sleeve into the affected blood vessel via an artery in the wrist or groin.

As a radiologist reviewing the videos of the cardiologist's procedure, he was ensuring a form of quality control, confirming the angiogram was interpreted correctly, and the angioplasty, if performed, was clinically warranted.

Of course, the obvious conundrum that arises from this process is a possible discrepancy between the opinion of the cardiologist, the heart specialist actually present at the procedure, and that of the radiologist, who specializes in expert interpretation of all kinds of x-rays, but provides an opinion in retrospect as opposed to real time. Nevertheless, this is the process and more often than not, the opinions complement each other.

Now, however, Harwick's review of the current angiogram left him scratching his head.

And he knew what he needed to do.

# CHAPTER TWENTY-ONE

Megan sat across the table from Art Kinkaid at Aldo's Trattoria. Kinkaid was making good on his promise of introducing her to the best Italian food in the area. What he didn't disclose, however, was that it was the only Italian restaurant this far west of Boston's North End.

She had just finished her meal of orecchiette with sausage al pesto, and he the Florentine steak. Now they were just chatting while they sipped what was left of a bottle of Chianti.

Up to this point, their conversation was confined to small talk and sharing tidbits of their non-medical backgrounds—hobbies, movie and reading genre likes and dislikes, favorite sports and such. She found him interesting and affable—until now, as he ventured into a topic that Megan considered a nonstarter.

"What was it like in D.C.?" he asked. "I mean, what you and your aunt went through during that entire FDA drama."

Feeling a sudden dryness in her throat and a queasy tightening sensation in the pit of her stomach, Megan responded haltingly. "You can read everything you need to know in the appropriate news articles. It's a topic I'd rather not discuss."

"Fine," he said. "Perhaps another time"

"No! not just tonight, not ever!"

"I'm sorry, Megan. I didn't mean to upset you. I imagine it was a pretty harrowing experience, so I can understand your reticence to discuss it. Unfortunately, I let curiosity get the better of me. We can just let it go."

*Thank goodness* "I appreciate that." she said.

He waved the waitress over for the check, and Allisyn took advantage of the break in their conversation. "Has Kacie Brendt spoken with you in regard to some concerns she has about the new EMR system?"

He raised his eyebrows and looked away from the waitress as he handed her his credit card, appearing taken aback by the question. When he finished paying the bill, he looked back over at Megan. "Are you referring to some inconsistencies she apparently noted in the medical record?"

"Uh-huh. But also the results of tests she insists she hadn't ordered herself."

"Yes, she did mention something about that. Did someone else order them?"

She shook her head. "Actually, she asked Ty Prendersen to look into it for her. According to him, all the tests in question were ordered into the EMR under her log-in ID."

"Hmm. Perhaps she just forgot ordering them."

"That's what Prendersen also said, although she insists she didn't. I was wondering if you could check into it for her."

He hesitated for a moment. "Sure. I'll double back with him to see if there's a more reasonable explanation for this and get back to her. I'll let you know as well." He paused as if in thought. "What were the tests for, anyway?"

"All genetic screening, unrelated to what Kacie was treating the patients for."

He leaned back in his chair. "Even more curious."

The waitress returned with his card and receipt, and they both rose to leave.

"Thank you for a wonderful meal, Art," she said. "It definitely met my high expectations given your enthusiastic recommendation."

He smiled warmly. "You're most welcome, Megan. Say, there's this nice little lounge with soft jazz not far from here. Join me for a nightcap?"

Taken off guard and not looking for a romantic entanglement, she didn't know how to respond. *On the other hand, aside from the discussion about Kacie's testing issue, it's been a pretty enjoyable evening and he's been good company. Besides, I'm off duty tomorrow and one drink won't hurt.*

Megan smiled. "Sounds delightful." As they walked out, she wished she had more clarity about Kacie's test ordering situation.

# CHAPTER TWENTY–TWO

"Come on in, Kacie." said Mitch Harwick.

Normally, it would be the clinician who would come to the radiologist to discuss x-ray films together, and since Kacie was no different, she quickly became well known to Harwick.

Today, however, was different. After reviewing the cardiac angiogram of one of Kacie's patients, the one he had puzzled over the day before, he asked her to come in to discuss his thoughts.

"Thanks for stopping by. I'd like to discuss a patient of yours."

He went on to provide the patient's name and describe his concern about her angiogram findings as they related to her clinical findings.

"What were her presenting symptoms?" he asked.

Kacie sat up straight in her chair. "She came in with some chest pain and shortness of breath. Her EKG showed some ischemic changes, so we treated her accordingly. Even though at forty-five she's kinda young for cardiac disease, I decided to proceed with a cardiology consult. Dr. Quinne saw her and recommended an angiogram."

"And what did he say it showed?"

"Several areas of coronary artery narrowing suggesting plaque buildup."

"And what did he propose for treatment?

Kacie hesitated, her forehead slightly wrinkled and eyes narrowed.

After a prolonged pause, she broke the silence. "I'm sorry, Mitch, but what are you getting at?"

"Let me try to phrase this…uh, delicately, Kacie. " He shifted in his chair. "I've reviewed all of Dr. Quinne's angiograms since he started here—and that's a lot of studies—so I think I have a good feel for his treatment recommendations. And based on what I've seen, I'd say he has a very low threshold for stent placement. In fact, most patients get at least one. Quite frankly, the fact that he didn't perform an angioplasty and stent placement to improve the blood flow in your patient here was quite perplexing for me, since he's placed stents in a good number of patients whose angiograms look a lot better than hers. So, I wanted to discuss her clinical history with you to better understand why not her."

Kacie leaned forward as if she was about to speak, but then pulled back.

Harwick picked up on her reticence to provide more detail. "You were going to say?"

She chewed on her lower lip "Look, Mitch, far be it from me to question a specialist's recommendations, especially when it comes to surgery or other invasive procedures, so I didn't want to countermand his treatment plan. But to be honest, I was pretty surprised myself that he recommended only medical treatment for this patient, despite her age. And I'm quite worried about her. She has somewhat of an unstable home situation—several small children and a job to support them, since she's separated from her husband. If that's not a setup for anxiety-related cardiac stress, I don't know what is. Between you and me, I think she should have angioplasty and a stent. What about you?"

He nodded. "I agree. Which is why I wanted to discuss it with you, to see if there's any reason the procedure is contraindicated in her case, and if not, what his reason was for not intervening. Any idea?"

Kacie looked down at her hands folded in her lap without responding.

"Kacie? Are you okay?"

Now she was wringing her hands. "Insurance."

"Huh?"

"She doesn't have insurance to cover the cost of the procedure, nor the wherewithal to pay out of pocket."

"What?" he said in a loud voice. "Are you saying he denied this patient appropriate treatment for financial reasons?"

She felt her face flush. "He didn't say so directly. Only to let him know when she does have adequate insurance to cover the procedure, and to maintain medical management until then."

He shook his head. "That's unbelievable."

"What can I say? I'm in no position to challenge him here."

"Yeah, well, I am. I'll give him a call and discuss it. Besides, I have some issues with a significant number of his other cases. Like I said, it's a rare patient of his that doesn't get a stent since his criteria are so low." He paused, sensing some discomfort on her part. "You okay, Kacie?"

She just nodded.

"Good. I'll let you know what he says. In the meantime, keep a close eye on the patient to make sure her symptoms don't worsen."

"Uh-huh. That's my plan."

She rose to leave. "Thanks for looking into this, Mitch. I didn't know exactly what approach to take. It's kind of sensitive, ya know?"

"Yeah, I sure do. I'll be in touch."

After she left, Harwick called Quinne's office and left a message for the cardiologist to get back to him as soon as possible.

Then he hung up, shaking his head.

# CHAPTER TWENTY–THREE

Trevor Quinne had not been in to see Harwick personally since the cardiologist's arrival at WGH to oversee the newly revived interventional cardiology program. As a radiologist and chief of the department, Harwick considered this pretty unusual, since reviewing x-rays and videos of interventional procedures—such as cardiac catheterization—with the radiologist for another opinion is a common practice among specialists.

So, when Quinne returned his call, Harwick had no illusions that getting him to do just that would be an easy task. And he wasn't dissuaded otherwise.

"Thanks' for getting back to me, Trevor. I"

"Yeah, well, I'm between cases and don't have much time. So, what's up?"

Harwick hesitated, taken aback by the brusque response. "I'd like to review a few of your angiograms together. and—"

"Review? What exactly do you mean?"

"Exactly that. Look at the angiograms together."

"What, are you questioning my reports?

Harwick sensed a definite edge in his voice. "No, I just want to make sure—"

"Are you implying I misread the studies?"

"You don't have to get defensive about this, Trevor. Peer review is standard practice."

"Yeah, well, I'm the cardiologist doing the procedure and you're a radiologist. That doesn't seem like a review by peers in my book."

Harwick sighed. He was stunned and didn't quite know how to respond. "Look, this is standard protocol, okay? Should I get Dr. Kinkaid involved?"

Quinne's scoff was clearly audible. "Don't bother. When do you want me to come by?"

"What's good for you?"

"I have one case left today. I'll stop by when I'm done. I should be able to be there in less than two hours. Does that work for you?"

Harwick confirmed it was acceptable, and the call ended. He was even more concerned now than when he spoke with Kacie, and anticipated a less than amicable meeting.

———

True to his word, Quinne arrived at Harwick's office ten minutes shy of two hours later. Harwick had a number of the cardiologist's cardiac cath videos prepared on screen, including the patient he had discussed with Kacie.

"Have a seat, Trevor," said Harwick. "I really appreciate you coming by, especially on such short notice."

Quinne shrugged. "No problem. Let's just get this over with."

"Thanks. I'd like to start with one patient that Dr. Brendt brought to my attention."

"Kacie Brendt?"

"Yes."

"Hmm. Doesn't surprise me."

Eyebrows raised, Harwick tilted his head to the side. "How so?"

"Let's just say we had a little professional disagreement about a certain patient's management—I suspect it's the one you're referring to."

"Let's see." Harwick pulled up the video of Kacie's patient identified by number for confidentiality.

Before he could say anything, Quinne jumped in. "Yep. — That's it."

"What was the disagreement?"

"I recommended medical treatment and she felt I should stent her. Is that what she told you?"

Harwick hesitated briefly. "She said you didn't proceed with intervention because she didn't have insurance, and—"

"What?" Quinne's jaw was set, and his eyes wide. "Are you serious? What a misrepresentation! In my opinion, and given her relatively young age and mild symptoms, I felt this patient should be managed medically with close observation, and stent placement was overtreatment. It had nothing to do with insurance or lack thereof."

"Why would Kacie make such an accusation? I'm sure I didn't misunderstand her."

"I have no idea. What I can say is she's a little overconfident with respect to her knowledge given her level of experience when it comes to specialty care. Thinks she knows it all and is appropriately experienced when interacting with specialists. Why she would make an issue of this is beyond me. What I can tell you is that I stand by my recommendation, for medical, not financial, reasons. Now, what are the other studies you want to review with me?"

After hesitating slightly to absorb the cardiologist's explanation, Harwick produced a list of patient names and corresponding ID numbers and handed it to him. "These patients were all stented by you, and I don't believe that was justified by the degree of obstruction seen on the cath video."

"So, now it's you questioning my clinical judgement? Are you saying I was inappropriately aggressive in placing stents?

Harwick stared at Quinne before speaking. "They were all referred in from one of the hospital's cardiac fairs, and symptoms were mild to moderate."

"What does where they were referred from have to do with their treatment? Like I said earlier, I'm the treating cardiologist who recommended and performed stent placement, you're the nonclinical radiologist and this discussion is nothing like standard peer review."

"We can always get an outside peer review organization," said Harwick. "I'm sure your professional organization can make recommendations. Or even the state can do a review and—"

"That's it, I'm outta here." Quinne stood and abruptly left.

Harwick just sat there, trying to digest what just occurred, and whether to share it with Art Kinkaid.

As soon as Quinne reached his car, he texted Oskar Wernuk on his cell.

*I think we have a problem.*

# CHAPTER TWENTY-FOUR

Megan and Kacie were back at the Campus Pub early on a Friday evening for what had become a regular week-ending ritual when both were off shift until the following Monday.

"So how was your date with Art Kinkaid?" asked Kacie.

Megan reddened. "I already told you it wasn't a date!"

"No? Dinner at one of the best restaurants in this town isn't a date?"

"Come on, knock it off, girl. It was just part of that getting to know you thing you said he does with everyone new."

"Yeah, well, I never got the restaurant treatment. So, what did you talk about?"

"Food."

"Food? What's with that?"

"He hardly knows anything about Italian cuisine, so I talked a little about it. Brainless small talk, ya know?"

"Hmm."

Megan took a sip of her beer, then poured a little more for each of them. "Actually, we also talked about you a good bit."

Kacie shifted uncomfortably in her seat. "Me? Seriously? What about?"

"Well, not you exactly. I asked him what he thought of your issue with the EMR and test ordering and…"

"And what? What did he say? I want to know."

"Easy, Kace. Hold on. He asked if someone else ordered them. When I told him you ran it by Prendersen, who told you the EMR showed them ordered under your ID, Art suggested you possibly got busy and simply forgot doing it, and—"

"That's pure BS, Megan, and you know it. There's also the issue of wrong diagnoses being assigned to some patients. I'm telling you, something screwy is happening with this new EMR."

"I haven't seen this happening myself, Kacie, but I guess it's possible the system is acting screwy. Anyway, he said he would get Prendersen to look into it more closely, so I guess we'll have to wait and see. Let's get the check."

Kacie put her hand on Megan's raised arm and gently pulled it down "Wait, I have a question. Do you have any experience with Trevor Quinne?

Megan looked up at her with raised eyebrows. "The new cardiologist?"

"Uh-huh. Have you had any patients treated by him? Specifically had a cardiac cath?"

"Not that I can recall. Why?"

Kacie proceeded to describe her recent discussion with Mitch Harwick about her patient, as well as the radiologist's opinion that Quinne was overly aggressive in his use of inappropriate invasive cardiac procedures.

Megan tilted her head. "Hmm. How about peer review of his cases?"

Kacie shook her head slightly. "Quinne is the only interventional cardiologist on staff."

Megan nodded. "Yeah, but an independent outside review can always be arranged. Has Mitch thought of that?"

"Not sure, although in my experience with Quinne, limited as it is, he's not going to look kindly on that suggestion."

Megan shrugged "Then I guess Mitch can discuss it with Kinkaid."

They finished their beer, paid the bill, and left in separate cars.

As much as she tried during the drive to her apartment, Megan couldn't make any sense of what was happening.

*Screwy sure is the right word. I'd rather think about how comfortable my dinner date was with Art Kinkaid. Could this be the beginning of something more?*

# CHAPTER TWENTY-FIVE

Trevor Quinne finished describing his confrontation with Mitch Harwick over Quinne's cardiac angiograms and stent placements to Ty Prendersen and Oskar Wernuk.

"You brought me here to resurrect your inactive interventional cardiology program and generate revenue for the hospital. To do that I need volume. And for that I need to work on the fringe. Now I have a do-good radiologist questioning my clinical decisions. I certainly don't need his threat of taking these cases, and me, to some mickey mouse peer review committee. After all, I'm the only interventional cardiologist in this damn place, so who the hell's my peer anyway?"

He paused while Prendersen and Wernuk silently looked at each other, then resumed. "Besides, before you know it, he'll get the state regulators involved, and that won't affect only me. You'll all be dragged into it as well. No way around it.—His threat needs to be eliminated. So, take care of it. And I don't care how." Then he abruptly left without saying another word.

Prendersen stood up. "I'll call our associate and make sure it's taken care of."

"Good." said Wernuk. "While you're at it, see what he suggests about that lady doctor you told me about causing trouble. You know, the one questioning all the patient information in their records. The way I see it, so far, she's just questioning the medical records. But before you know it, she's going to put it all together. And that'll cause a whole lot of pain for all of us. Besides, Quinne is pretty hot under the collar about her as well. Apparently, she questioned his treatment of one of her patients and shared that with Harwick, which pissed Quinne off big time. And we can't afford to lose his revenue stream. I suspect she's going to be a problem one way or the other going forward. Either just a pain in the ass annoyance, or a dangerous whistleblower if she figures things out. Either way, we'll have to deal with her sooner or later, so might as well be now."

"Mm-hmm. I'll take care of it." Then Prendersen left, leaving Wernuk sitting at the table, tapping his fingers on the surface. He took out his phone and scrolled through the contact list.

When he reached the one he was looking for, he tapped the screen to dial the number, and spoke when it was answered. "We have some complications to take care of."

# CHAPTER TWENTY–SIX

"Damn!" said Elsbeth Sentini, dropping her phone onto the bedside table. She had finished showering when her phone rang, and she took the call sitting on her side of the bed with only a towel wrapped around her head.

Wendell Courte was standing on the other side of the bed, just beginning to get dressed. They had spent the night together once again, neither getting much sleep,

"Problems?"

"Apparently so." She turned to face him. That was Wernuk over at WGH."

"Anything I can help with?"

"Not really. You did your job in getting the state regulators to approve resumption of the interventional cardiology program. And Trevor Quinne has done a great job ramping up cases with the help of referrals from the community heart fairs. Volume has been steadily increasing, and that's been a huge revenue boost."

"So, what's the problem?"

"The chief of radiology, a fellow by the name of Harwick, has been reviewing all the cardiac angiograms, and he seems to think Quinne is overly aggressive, and placing stents inappropriately."

"What the hell? Just tell the radiologist to stick to reading simple x-rays."

"Huh! If only it were that simple. Unfortunately, there's more to it. He wants Quinne's cases peer reviewed. Since he's the only interventional cardiologist on the staff, that would require an outside consultant to perform a review of Quinne's cases, which could go south really quick. He's even threatening to alert the state regulators, which would likely trigger a full audit of the program by the state, and possibly even federal officials."

"Whoa! That wouldn't be very pretty. And my political credibility would likely take a real hit as well. What're they planning to do about it?"

"Don't know. Probably add by subtraction."

"Huh?"

"Keep adding more cases and subtract the threat of outside review."

Courte shook his head and held up his hand in a stop gesture. "That's all I need to know. Keep me out of it."

She chuckled. "Don't worry, I can't afford to lose my most valuable political connection." She unraveled the towel from her head and dropped it on the floor. Naked, she crawled on the bed over to him, unbuttoned his shirt, loosened his belt, and pulled him down to her.

When finished, they both dressed and left together, but traveling cautiously in different directions. The nighttime snow and ice had left the roads slippery and treacherous.

# CHAPTER TWENTY–SEVEN

The man Oskar Wernuk had referred to as "our associate" was standing outside in the driveway of Mitch Harwick's house dressed in black slacks and hooded sweatshirt, with heavy black shoes—virtually invisible to the keenest of eyes given the darkness of night.

With a sordid background as a mercenary, he was willing to take on the most despicable—and illegal—requests of his clients, preferring to be thought of as a "fixer," discretely solving problems for a premium fee. And he was thinking how this one hit the jackpot. "A twofer," he muttered under his breath, as he was about to solve the first of two problems he had been asked to fix by Ty Prendersen.

Harwick lived near the top of a large hill, the steep drive down to the main highway leading to the hospital a daunting trip in the best of weather. Despite the hazard, his fondness for the spectacular view of the valley below remained undeterred. On a cold winter's night like this, however, the driveway was exceptionally precarious, given the snow and ice-covered surface, and a deadly precipice lurking below guarded by a tenuous embankment.

The man in black waited until the house lights went out, confident he was virtually invisible in the darkness. He crouched beside Harwick's all-wheel drive sport utility vehicle, carefully inspected its chassis with a focused light, and set to his task. When finished to his satisfaction, he slid down the steep, slippery driveway, leaving no sign he was there by covering his tracks on the way down with fresh snow. When he reached the bottom, he made one additional alteration across the street and drove off in his car, unnoticed by any living creature, except perhaps the night owl in a nearby tree. His thoughts quickly turned to the second problem he was being paid to fix.

# CHAPTER TWENTY–EIGHT

"Thanks for taking the time to meet on a weekend," said Art Kinkaid. He had invited Megan to join him for breakfast at a local diner on a Saturday morning when she wasn't working.

She responded only with a tight-lipped smile and nodded her head.

Kinkaid ignored her non-verbal response. "I thought it would be good to have this discussion outside our work environment."

She took a deep breath. "You said it was about Kacie. Is there a problem?"

"No, not really. At least I certainly hope not."

"Hmm. Sounds a little disconcerting. Mind being a little more specific?"

Kinkaid took a sip of coffee and leaned forward closer to her. "It seems she's still fixated on this medical record issue. In fact, she's continued to meet with Ty Prendersen intermittently and urging him to investigate more about tests she didn't order and chart notes with diagnoses she doesn't recall making. She even suggested an outside review of the EMR to him, which won't go over well with Regnant, since it's their proprietary system. To be honest, Megan, I'm a little worried about her. I don't want to go into the entire issue of physician burnout, but I'm concerned about her being a little depressed. Have you noticed anything like that?"

"Uh, I wouldn't say depressed. Obsessed is a little more like it. She's quite emphatic about the subject when we talk about it."

"I see." He paused, seemingly in deep thought. "From the time she first came to work here, I considered her…well, not exactly withdrawn or reclusive. Perhaps private is the right word. Which is why I wanted to have this discussion with you. It seems you've bonded with each other well, and I thought you could shed some light on her state of mind."

Uncomfortable with the direction this conversation seemed to be taking, Megan shifted in her seat. "Uh, I don't know if that's"

"Don't get me wrong, Megan. I don't mean to pry into your relationship with Kacie, but do you think she'd be open to speaking with one of our behavioral therapists? I really wouldn't want to see her digress into a full-blown depression. " … "I know how difficult it was for you with your friend in Baltimore, and none of us would want to see anything like that happen here. And not to be presumptuous, but I thought you could provide some insight as to whether she would consider such therapy."

She didn't respond.

"I'm sorry, Megan. I didn't mean to upset you. Are you okay?"

She took a deep breath and sighed. "I appreciate your concern for Kacie's emotional well-being, Art, but I can't really say. She's so convinced there's something funky about this EMR."

"I see. Would you consider bringing the subject of some professional help up with her?

Megan shrugged and frowned slightly. "I don't know, Art. I can certainly talk with her and see if she might consider it. She's quite headstrong, though."

"I totally understand," he said, waving his hand for the waitress.

They finished up and headed outside to their cars. As they each drove off slowly, the road slippery from the cover of snow and ice, both their cellphones chimed with a text message.

There was an urgent situation at the hospital. Mitch Harwick had been in a serious car accident.

# CHAPTER TWENTY–NINE

When Art Kinkaid arrived at the hospital following his breakfast meeting with Megan, he went directly to his office. Penny Salicio was already there, standing at her desk and talking on the phone. She held up her free hand, extending her forefinger, signaling him to wait a minute. Her attire was clearly casual and she looked a little disheveled. Kinkaid gave her a mental pass on her appearance since it was the weekend and she was undoubtedly there only because of the urgency of the situation.

She finished the call, dropping the phone and letting it dangle by the chord as she stared straight ahead, not addressing her boss.

"How's Mitch?" asked Kinkaid.

Remaining silent, she continued to stare straight ahead without turning toward him. When she finally spoke, her voice was raspy and it sounded like she was choking back a sob. "He's dead."

Kinkaid immediately walked over to her, turned her toward him and held her in a tight embrace, her tears wet on his shirt.

# CHAPTER THIRTY

"What the hell happened?" bellowed Megan as she burst into the physician lounge. Kacie was there alone, waiting for Megan after she had texted her that Mitch Harwick had died in a car accident.

Kacie was talking on the phone but offered a hurried goodbye and abruptly disconnected when she eyed Megan, then sighed deeply and collapsed in a chair.

"That was Penny Salicio on the phone. Not a lot of details, but she knows that Mitch's house is on a hill with a steep driveway down to the main drag, where there's a barrier placed on the opposite side of the road to prevent anyone from driving off what is a long drop. Why he would want to live there is anyone's guess. Anyway, it's a hairy drive down the hill under the best of conditions. Unfortunately, the snow and ice today made it even more treacherous. As best as the police can tell, his car slid down the driveway, crossed the main road, went through the barrier on the other side and right down the steep drop. Apparently, the car was really mangled when they arrived, and Mitch had to be extracted." She stopped for a moment, then continued in a quavering voice. "He must have had severe injuries, because he died in the ambulance on the way to Johnson Trauma Center."

"Trauma center?" Megan had a puzzled look on her face. "Why didn't they bring him here?"

"The trauma center was closer."

Megan sat next to Kacie, placing an arm around her shoulder, and pulled her close, noting her friend's eyes were clouded by tears.

"That's terrible, Kacie. I'm so sorry. I know you were both fond of each other."

Head down, hands folded in her lap, Kacie didn't reply, and they both sat there in silence. After several minutes, which seemed like an eternity to Megan, she placed a hand under Kacie's chin and gently lifted her head, their eyes meeting in mutual anguish. It was then that she recalled her recent discussion with Art Kinkaid about Kacie's mental and emotional state.

"Are you okay?" asked Megan"

Kacie tilted her head and looked at Megan, eyes questioning. "Huh?"

Megan wondered if it was the best time to broach the subject, but quickly decided to proceed. "Emotionally, I mean. You've been pretty upset with all the EMR issues, and now this. You must be rather distressed."

Kacie frowned. "Emotionally? Distressed? What are you getting at?"

Megan sighed. "I don't know, Kace. With all that's gone on, I'm just worried about you, how you're holding up mentally, and—"

"Holding up mentally?" Kacie's frown deepened into a scowl and her voice raised. "Are you serious? Questioning my emotional stability? " She paused, breathing heavily. "Our colleague and a good friend just died. How the hell do you expect me to feel?"

"I don't know. I'm sorry. I didn't mean to upset you. It's just that—"

"I'm not like Agacia, if that's what you're worried about."

Megan snapped her head back and looked at her sharply. "That's a little harsh, Kacie, don't you think? You know how distraught I was over her death. And I don't want to see anything close to that with you." She lowered her eyes and bowed her head, sniffling softly.

"Sorry, Megan. That was unfair of me. I didn't mean to trivialize your feelings for Agacia and downplay her death."

"It's okay, Kace. I just don't want to see you go through that same kind of emotional torment. Have you considered getting some counseling? You know, help you deal with all the frustration related to the EMR issue. And now this terrible event piled on top of it all. Some therapy could help you put it all in perspective and alleviate the stress of this emotional turmoil."

Kacie remained silent.

Megan persisted "Kace? Have you thought about that?"

"Not really. Sure, the EMR issue has been frustrating, but I wouldn't say I'm burned out or depressed because of it. I am curious, though, over what's going on. Aren't you?

Megan sighed. "Yeah, I guess."

Kacie's shoulders sagged. "It's been stressful, Meg. Staff morale has really been in the dumps since the firing of Alan Fresney from the CEO position. He was well-liked around here, and it came completely out of the blue with no explanation why. A real jolt to the system. And now this with Mitch. Seriously, though, I really don't feel emotionally off-balance. And certainly not depressed to the point of needing a therapist."

Megan gave her a weak smile. "You'll be sure to let me know if you feel it's getting out of hand, right? And consider some help managing it?" Kacie returned the smile and nodded. "Will do. And thanks for being such a good and caring friend."

Megan stood, encouraging Kacie to follow by gently pulling up on her elbow. "Let's go for a little walk, Kace. Some fresh air will do us both some good."

They walked off together in search of some respite from the grief they were sharing.

# CHAPTER THIRTY-ONE

An emotional memorial service for Mitch Harwick was held one week following his unfortunate demise, attended by as many hospital staff as possible without jeopardizing safe patient care, bolstered by a cadre of locum tenens physicians and nurses to ensure that goal.

Other than his estranged wife from whom he was separated without children, no other family members were present, although a good number of non-medically related friends attended.

Megan and Kacie sat side by side, occasionally clutching each other's hand.

Eulogies were delivered by Art Kinkaid and Elsbeth Sentini, lauding Harwick as an exceptional practitioner in his specialty and for his professional interactions with colleagues. Oskar Wernuk and Ty Prendersen were conspicuously absent.

Back at the hospital, the WGH staff was still reeling from the horrible event. It seemed everyone was in a state of disbelief, going about their daily routines and limiting their verbal interactions with others to patients and communications necessary for effective clinical care.

A police investigation of the accident scene, including Harwick's car, was ongoing, but the evidence so far indicated a failure of the brakes to effectively counter the extreme icy and snow-covered condition of the steep driveway, and the failure of the barrier on the opposite side of the highway to prevent the car from careening down the precipice below. It was clearly fortunate another vehicle was not passing by at the exact same time the car crossed the road, averting an even more disastrous event. When the service concluded, there was a short period of attendees milling around, sharing stories and experiences about Harwick. In due time, the gathering dispersed and those with hospital duties left to carry them on.

# CHAPTER THIRTY-TWO

Following Harwick's memorial service, Art Kinkaid and Elsbeth Sentini returned to the hospital for a meeting with Oskar Wernuk and Ty Prendersen to discuss recruitment of a replacement for the position of radiology department chairperson. They all agreed this was a crucial recruitment and should not devolve into a lengthy process. With his extensive list of contacts cultivated from his past engagements, Wernuk offered to spearhead the recruitment with oversight from Kinkaid as medical director. His offer was accepted by all, and the group disbanded to attend to their various obligations.

When the others left, Kinkaid realized he hadn't eaten all day, so he headed over to the cafeteria. He grabbed a sandwich and soft drink and was about return to his office and eat at his desk when he spotted Megan sitting alone, and went over to her table. "Mind if I join you?"

"Not at all," she said. "Please do."

He pulled up a chair. "How are you holding up?"

"About as well as can be expected. Like everyone else, I guess."

He nodded with a subtle frown. "Did you ever speak with Kacie about what we discussed? You know, about getting some counseling."

She was about to bite into her sandwich, but stopped and put it down. Yes, I did." She picked up the sandwich again and took a bite.

"And?"

She sighed and put the sandwich down again. "I guess I'm not going to finish this gourmet lunch."

He shrugged and winced slightly. "Sorry. That was rather inconsiderate of me."

She pushed the plate away and wiped her hands with a napkin. "Not to worry. It isn't very good anyway." She took a sip of water, and leaned back in her chair.

He waited only briefly before continuing to press for a response. "So? How did it go? with Kacie"

Megan sighed again. "She felt she wasn't at all depressed and didn't need any counseling or other such support, only an explanation of what's happening with the EMR.

He folded his arms and leaned back. "You do know that clinical depression is frequently not recognized by individuals who suffer from it, right? Or they do realize it, but are in denial about how it affects them?"

Megan shifted in her seat and glared at him indignantly. "Of course, I know that!"

"Well, then perhaps—"

"Well then nothing! Look, she's frustrated, annoyed and irate."

Kinkaid sneered. "Frustrated and irate? At what?"

"Seriously? You must be kidding!" . . . "About everyone's dismissal of her observations regarding the issues with the EMR and the administration's failure to do anything about it." "No one seems to take her seriously. And apparently, I'm afraid that includes you. Quite frankly, I'd be more than a little pissed off myself if I was treated so indifferently."

Kinkaid leaned his elbow on the table and stroked his chin. "I see. Well, perhaps I need to speak with our friend Prendersen again and maybe light a fire under him to check things out in more detail. After all, its Regnant's system we're dealing with, and he should know it inside out."

"That would be great, Art. Thanks for offering to intervene with him."

"Sure, Megan. No problem. That's the least I can do to get this issue sorted out and corrected, since I'm no computer system whizz myself." He paused briefly, in thought. "But I'd still keep an eye on her for any signs that might suggest clinical depression."

Megan nodded. "Will do, Art. Don't get me wrong, I appreciate your interest in her wellbeing. It's just that I'm pretty sensitive to her situation after the death of my friend Agacia under similar circumstances. Thanks for talking to Prendersen. I'm sure it will make her feel supported by clinical leadership."

"Certainly. We physicians need to stick together." he said with a smile.

They both stood, bussed their trays and went in different directions. Off to round on her patients, Megan immediately called Kacie to let her know the good news about Kinkaid's pledge to speak with Prendersen about resolving the EMR issue once and for all.

When Kinkaid reached his office, as promised he called Ty Prendersen. But instead of the EMR issue, it was about a related problem.

# CHAPTER THIRTY-THREE

Kacie was emotionally and physically exhausted the morning after a busy night shift at the hospital following Harwick's memorial service the day before. She pulled into the parking lot of her apartment building and was disappointed to see her favorite space close to the entrance was taken. "Dammit," she said. "Of all nights for someone to pick this spot, especially when my legs feel like rubber."

Then her thoughts quickly reverted to the encouraging phone call from Megan during the night. She was apparently successful in getting Art Kinkaid to work with Prendersen right away to straighten out the frustrating EMR issue. Her spirits boosted by the news, she shook off her annoyance at her favored parking spot being occupied, and eased into the next closest space she could find. She slowly walked over to the building entrance and unlocked the common front door. As she approached the elevator in the empty building lobby, she couldn't place it, but she felt overwhelmed by an uneasy feeling. *Must be exhaustion from barely getting any sleep last night,* she thought while waiting for the elevator. When she arrived at the fourth floor, she looked down the hallway in both directions. Noting it was empty and otherwise unremarkable, she took a deep breath and sighed. She walked briskly to her apartment, unlocked the door, and entered. Flipping on the light, she scanned the space and likewise saw nothing unusual—until she tried to close the door. That's when she looked down and saw the front end of a black shoe wedged between the door jamb and the door, preventing it from closing.

# CHAPTER THIRTY-FOUR

"Have you seen Dr. Brendt?" said Penny Salicio over the phone.

"Kacie?" said Megan, ignoring Penny's formality. "Why? What's up?"

"She wasn't at her rounds this morning and she's not answering her phone."

"Hmm. How about checking with HR to see if she logged in yet today."

"Did that too. Negative. I know she had the overnight shift after Dr. Harwick's memorial service. Perhaps she's just exhausted between the two and catching up on her sleep."

"Possibly, Penny, but that isn't like her at all. I mean not to let anyone know she would be in late. It just seems strange, that's all." Megan paused, silently admonishing herself. I *wonder if Kinkaid was right about the depression issue, and she's gone and done something rash.* "If I can get someone to cover my patients, I'll take a quick trip over to her place and see what's up."

"Good idea," said Penny. "I'll check the roster and get someone to cover for you."

"Thanks. And I'll give you a call back when I get there and know something."

"Sounds good. I'll be right here waiting," said Penny.

Megan was about to disconnect the call when she stopped. "Oh, one more thing. Be sure to let Dr. Kinkaid know."

"Of course." When the call ended, Penny dialed Kinkaid's number, her steady hand belying her innermost apprehension.

# CHAPTER THIRTY-FIVE

On the drive to Kacie's apartment, Megan couldn't stop thinking of Art Kinkaid's comments about depression. She felt a growing uneasy sensation in the pit of her stomach and her hands began to tremble as she approached the building. She went to the parking space Kacie always jokingly referred to as "hers," but it was occupied by another car. Her uneasy feeling escalated, and she now bordered on outright nausea. When she finally spotted Kacie's car, it was empty and the doors were locked. Through the window, she could see Kacie's white jacket with a stethoscope in one pocket on the front passenger seat.

Megan walked over to the building's front door, anxious to see if she could enter. It wasn't locked and she went in freely. Familiar with Kacie's apartment from frequent visits for occasional non-work talk sessions, she took the elevator to the fourth floor. Before walking down the hall to the apartment, she stopped and tried to reach Kacie by phone one more time, but came up empty. So, she walked to the apartment and knocked on the door. No response. She knocked again, now hard enough to generate a louder noise on the chance Kacie was in a distant part of the apartment or sleeping. Again, no response, except this time it was evident the door was not locked or even fully closed, as it gently swung inward from the force, although not far enough to look inside. Her view was still partially obstructed by the half-opened door, but she could see the room was lit with a soft glow. Her apprehension rising, she shook off a tremor that had temporarily abated, but now returned. She pushed the door further inward, averting her gaze inside.

# CHAPTER THIRTY–SIX

With the door to Kacie's apartment fully open, Megan hesitated at the threshold and scanned the dimly lit room, which appeared undisturbed. She called out Kacie's name, but there was no response. She slowly entered, approaching a sofa in the middle of the room that was situated with its back to the door, blocking a view of the other side of the room. As she came up aside the sofa, she saw the seating covered by a blanket, bulging as if it was covering something underneath. She briefly hesitated, then gently pressed down on the blanket, noting its softness. She pealed back the blanket, and let out a sigh of relief when she saw what lie beneath were only several throw pillows. She continued to move from one room to the other, calling out Kacie's name as she did, but there was still no response. As she approached the doorway of the last of the rooms, the bedroom, she felt that queasiness in the pit of her stomach once again. The door to the room was open, but the lights were off and the darkness precluded assessment of its contents.

When she found the light switch on the wall and flipped it on, she uttered a huge gasp and stepped back, almost falling over. Kacie was sprawled out on her back in the middle of the bed, eyes partially open but unseeing, and there was still no response when Megan again called out her name. She approached the bed with short, tentative steps and gently touched Kacie's arm. It was cool and didn't do as much as twitch at the contact.

She held Kacie's left wrist and checked for a pulse, but felt nothing. Then she leaned over with their faces nearly touching, and detected no evidence of even the shallowest of breathing. As she pulled away, Megan's own breathing became more labored and her eyes began to well up with tears. She brushed away the wetness, and looked down at Kacie once again. This time she noticed the opened pill bottle lying on the bed next to Kacie's opposite hand. The bottle was near empty with several pills scattered around it.

"Oh my god! "uttered Megan aloud as tears now freely flowed down her cheeks. Struggling to slow her breathing down, she took a deep breath and let out a loud sigh.

She called 911and began to resuscitate her friend. By the time rescue arrived and took over, Megan realized it was futile to continue. The thought that Art Kinkaid's caution about depression had become a reality was painfully unbearable for Megan to contemplate. Despite her anguish, however, she knew what she needed to do next and used her cell to call Kinkaid's number.

# CHAPTER THIRTY–SEVEN

Word of Kacie's death spread quickly throughout the staff of WGH. Although a police investigation was ongoing, the initial consensus by authorities was suicide, even though the autopsy and post-mortem blood studies were still pending, and a suicide note was never found.

As if staff morale wasn't low enough after Mitch Harwick's demise and Alan Fresney's dismissal as CEO, there was no doubt it was getting worse. At least Harwick's death was considered accidental. Suicide on the part of a staff member—a physician, no less—was devastating, however, and one shock too many to the organization.

Seven days after Megan's discovery of Kacie, the coroner's report officially designated Kacie's death a suicide by barbiturate overdose. And the working theory was she obtained the drug from the hospital formulary. The police had no evidence suggesting foul play, and after learning from Art Kinkaid about Kacie's obsession with the EMR issue, concluded the anxiety and depression related to it were the underlying factors that pushed her to such a drastic action.

To Kinkaid's credit, he never said "I told you so" to Megan or otherwise reference their discussions about Kacie before her death.

Although Megan never said so to him, she appreciated his discretion and avoidance of those earlier conversations.

# CHAPTER THIRTY-EIGHT

WGH held a memorial service for Kacie ten days after her death. A large number of hospital staff attended, leaving enough staff to manage the clinical duties at the hospital, with attendees on call as needed. Kacie grew up in a small town outside of Boston, and a significant number of family and friends were present as well. As with Harwick, several staff members provided eulogies, including Megan. She elaborated on how much Kacie meant to her as a colleague, mentor, and friend. Art Kinkaid spoke, praising her for her clinical acumen, collaboration with other clinical staff, and dedication to her patients. A surprise attendee was Elsbeth Sentini in her capacity as interim hospital CEO, although she didn't speak or stay for the short reception afterwards. Small groups gathered to share personal anecdotes regarding their interactions with Kacie. One specific topic, however, was never mentioned by anyone during the reception—Kacie's concerns about the EMR.

# CHAPTER THIRTY-NINE

Two weeks after Kacie's memorial service, Megan was still walking around as if in a fog. Agacia, Harwick and now Kacie. Three deaths at this point in her life were too much to bear. She couldn't make any sense of it.

Megan had assumed the care of Kacie's patients while still maintaining her own service. She thought the extra shifts would keep her busy and her mind off all that had transpired until some time had passed. Instead, whenever she had a difficult patient care issue, she couldn't keep herself from asking *What would Kacie do? What would Agacia do?* To make it even worse, any time she contemplated going to the campus pub for a brief respite, she couldn't pull it off. Memories of her regular sessions there with Kacie—times of camaraderie knocking around far-ranging topics—were simply too painful.

"I've got to do something to make sense of all this and keep my sanity." she chided herself out loud one evening, alone in her apartment as she sipped a glass of wine. *But what, exactly?*

She was about to freshen her drink with a small pour when she came to a decision.

# CHAPTER FORTY

The following morning was Thursday, and Megan arrived at the hospital well before the start of her patient rounds. Since she had assumed coverage of Kacie's inpatients, she had full access to their records in the EMR. Megan's plan was to review those records to see if she could corroborate Kacie's claim that certain diagnoses and tests ordered were not of her doing.

--------

After nearly two hours, Megan had to stop her review to round on her own patients. What she had seen so far, however, supported Kacie's assertion that there were numerous tests ordered not pertinent to many of her patients, and diagnoses often recorded that were not consistent with Kacie's documented history and physical exam. Unfortunately, however, Ty Prendersen's response that all the documentation and test orders were done under Kacie's own official log-in credentials was also correct. Which meant Kacie apparently did in fact order the tests and entered the documentation herself, not someone else. *Unless, of course, that someone else spuriously used Kacie's credentials to log in and make changes.* Now Megan was totally confused. *What the hell does all this mean?* She had no answer, and had to stop her review to care for her own patients, resolving to give it more thought later. Just then, her cell pinged with a text. It was from Penny Salicio. *A police detective is here and needs to speak with you.*

# CHAPTER FORTY-ONE

When Megan arrived in the executive suite, Penny Salicio was at her desk. She raised her head to look at Megan and pointed to the conference room's closed door. "She's waiting in there for you."

*"She?"* thought Megan as she opened the door, entered, and closed it behind her.

Sitting at the table was a serious looking woman whose understated business attire—

a gray jacket over white blouse and matching slacks, along with the absence of a police badge or other such visible identification, belied her status as a law enforcement agent.

That was quickly rectified when she stood, removed a leather wallet from her jacket pocket and opened it to show her badge, introducing herself as Detective Helen Backstrom.

"Doctor McLoren?"

Megan nodded. "Mm-hmm. Megan McLoren. What can I do for you, detective?" She sat at the table and Backstrom followed suit.

The detective replaced the badge into her pocket. "Doctor Kinkaid recommended I speak with you about Doctor Brendt."

Megan felt her throat tighten and she looked away from the detective without saying a word. Her breathing quickened and she held her hands together tightly as she leaned on the table.

Backstrom noted Megan's apparent discomfort, and hesitated briefly. "He said you and Kacie were quite close. Is that correct?"

Megan looked up at her with pursed lips and nodded.

"I'm sorry, Doctor. I know this must be difficult for you, but it's important to understand what happened to her."

Megan remained speechless, continuing to stare at the detective.

Despite Backstrom's empathy for Megan's emotional reaction, the detective was undeterred from her task. "Are you aware no suicide note was recovered from Kacie's apartment?"

Megan fidgeted with her hands on the table. "Yes."

Backstrom shifted in her seat. "Dr. Kinkaid said he had several discussions with you about Kacie's state of mind. Something about her being quite anxious and upset by problems with the hospital medical records—some discrepancies or other issues. And he was concerned about her mental and emotional state. He seemed to think she was suffering from a degree of anxiety and depression, and he asked you to keep an eye on her. Is that accurate"

Megan sighed and took a deep breath. "Uh-huh. He wanted me to try and get her to agree to some professional help in dealing with her emotional state."

"And how did she react to that?"

"She was pretty firm that she was not clinically depressed, and didn't need a psychiatrist or any other form of behavioral intervention."

Backstrom paused to write in a small notebook. "And what did you think about that?"

"What did I think? Seriously? I think she was legitimately disturbed at what was going on with the medical records, and nobody in administration seemed to give a damn. She was as frustrated as hell about it. Depressed? Suicidal? I didn't think so. Just pissed off."

Backstrom leaned forward and looked intensely at Megan. "Are you implying she didn't take her own life?"

"Hell no! I don't know what to think. Maybe it was just an accident, or maybe she was trying to calm herself down and unfortunately overdosed." Megan pounded a fist on the table. "All I know is this is the second close friend I've lost in a short period, and I can't deal with it." A few tears trickled down her face.

The detective stood up. "I think that's all for now. I don't have any other questions. I'm sorry for your loss, doctor, and for upsetting you."

"It's okay, detective. It's your job." Megan looked down and dabbed a tear off her cheek. with a tissue.

Backstrom slid her business card across the table over to her. "Please contact me if you think of anything else I should know." Then she left.

Megan was confused, and just sat there by herself, elbows on the table, head down in her hands. *What have I done? Did I misread the signs, or was I in denial and just didn't want to believe that Kacie was clinically depressed, and I simply misinterpreted her protests?* Megan's assumed guilt was palpable.

Just then the door opened. It was Penny. "Are you okay?"

Megan stood. "Okay as it gets," she said as she brushed by Penny to leave. "Now it's back to work."

# CHAPTER FORTY-TWO

After leaving Penny Salicio, Megan rounded on her patients and those of Kacie's whose care she had assumed. When finished, she was about to resume her review of Kacie's patient records in search of further discrepancies to support her friend's assertions when a thought made her stop in her tracks. *What about my own patients?*

She began reviewing the electronic records of all the patients on her service, including those she had since discharged, as well as those currently under her care. She stopped after two hours, confused. None of them had similar discrepancies in test ordering and diagnoses. It just didn't make sense. *Why Kacie's patients and not mine?* She had no reasonable answer, but that question led to another. *What about all the other patients in the hospital?*

She started the painfully laborious task of reviewing random records alphabetically, even though she knew it wasn't possible to do so for every patient. Interestingly, it didn't take long for her to recognize a trend. Although it was just a sample of random patients, every one of them exhibited the same discrepancies Kacie had described for her patients—various diagnoses that couldn't be explained by the physician's diagnostic findings, and tests ordered, always of the same type—genetic— that were extraneous to the patients' condition and physician findings. And in every case, the documented diagnosis and test orders were entered by the physician caring for the patient. Now Megan was really confused. There was no explanation for what was going on, and why she was an outlier. She decided to quit for the present time and give it more thought before resuming her search.

---

Meanwhile, some distance away from the hospital in the office of Regnant Health's administrative location, Elsbeth Sentini sat with Oskar Wernuk and Ty Prendersen, intently watching a computer screen that tracked and displayed in real time all of Megan's actions in the EMR."

"Dammit!" said Wernuk. "She's getting too close. I think she's gonna be more trouble than the other two."

"In that case," said Sentini. "I believe you need a contingency plan, something more subtle that won't get the attention of that detective. So, take care of it before she blows the whistle."

Without saying a word, Prendersen nodded and used his cell to dial the number for their associate, also referred to as "the fixer."

# CHAPTER FORTY-THREE

The following day was Friday, and as hospitalist on call to the ER, Megan anticipated it to be a busy one, as was typically the case for that assignment. Fortunately, she had no clinical shifts scheduled for Saturday or Sunday. With any luck, the ER would be quiet, allowing her to round on her patients and sign out to one of the other hospitalists on inpatient call for the remainder of the weekend. That would free her to devote a sizeable amount of time to reviewing additional records without inpatient care responsibilities slowing her down.

With that plan in mind, she arrived at the hospital at her typical early time and began her rounds so she would have the most up-to-date information to provide to the hospitalist on call for the weekend.

Megan had skipped breakfast, with only coffee on her ride in, and was on her way to the cafeteria for an early lunch when her cellphone pinged. It was Penny Salicio.

*What now?* and she called her right back.

Penny answered promptly. "Doctor Kinkaid would like you to join him here in his office for lunch. What would you like me to get you? He's ordering from the deli across the street."

Megan rolled her eyes. *At least that's better than the cafeteria!* "A pastrami on rye would be fine, Penny. What time?"

"It's 11:45 now, so let's say 12:30. That should give the deli plenty of time. I'll pick it up and have it here when you arrive."

Megan paused. "Sounds like a plan. Thanks for the invite."

"Don't mention it. You can thank Doctor Kinkaid when you get here."

Megan simply said "See ya then." And she left to check on several patients before heading over for lunch.

---

Megan arrived at the hospital executive suite promptly at 12:30. Penny was seated at her desk, phone held up to her ear while working on her computer. She looked up when Megan entered and placed her hand over the phone. "Grab a seat in the conference room. Lunch is already on the table. He's on a call but should be done shortly."

Megan was a little surprised by her informality, but didn't say a word. Instead, she entered the conference room, deliberately avoiding where she was seated for her meeting with the police detective. Nevertheless, a shiver ran down her spine as she recalled that conversation.

Within minutes, the door burst open and Kinkaid entered, pulling the door closed behind him.

Megan started to stand, but he raised his hand in a "stop" gesture. "Please don't get up, Megan. This is completely informal." He eyed the two bags holding their respective lunches, took the one with his name handwritten on it, and slid the other across the table to her.

He began unwrapping his sandwich as he spoke. "So, you met with Detective uh . . . Backstrom. Is that right?"

"Uh-huh." She nodded, ignoring her sandwich.

Kinkaid paused briefly to take a bite of his. And she told you about not being able to locate a note left by Kacie to explain her action?"

"Mm-hmm. But I already knew that since I never came across one either when I found her."

"Right. That's why I suggested to her that she meet with you, given your close relationship with Kacie." He took a small bite of his sandwich before continuing. "I thought what you and I discussed about her emotional state precipitated by her fixation with the EMR issue would help the police understand the role her state of mind played in harming herself as she did."

Megan was about to take a bite of her sandwich when she stopped abruptly and glowered at him. "In other words, you expected me to validate her depression—which Kacie repeatedly denied—as her motive for taking her own life?"

He put his half-eaten sandwich down and re-wrapped it. "Well, it's not unreasonable to believe her unrelenting anxiety and frustration over that situation eventually led to depression over her inability to control those feelings, and then to—"

"Huh!" Megan tossed her sandwich into the bag, slowly shook her head , and leaned back without saying anything more.

Noticing her reaction, Kinkaid paused before continuing "Unfortunately, that seems like the most logical way to look at this. And after speaking with you, Detective Backstrom is inclined to agree."

Megan's face reddened. "That's it, then? She simply committed suicide?"

"I'm sorry, Megan. I know you had become really close with Kacie, something I never saw with her and others before you arrived. Which is why I really wanted to have this conversation. You see, I've become quite fond of you myself. You're an excellent physician and clearly a wonderful individual and exceptional friend to have. All qualities I truly admire. And I don't want to see you spiral into a state of depression yourself over Kacie's unfortunate demise. You are a great asset to Wallberg General, and although your plan is to leave when appropriate to pursue your fellowship, I want you to know what value you provide to our community. Who knows? Maybe you'll even return as an infectious disease specialist after you complete your fellowship."

Megan sighed, a barely perceptible tear in her eye.

He reached across the table and took her hand, squeezing gently. "Listen, how about you and I make a return engagement to Aldo's Trattoria and get your mind off all this? Besides, I have a feeling there's a lot more about Italian cuisine—and wine—you can teach me. He paused. "What do you say? This weekend?"

She looked up with a half-smile and squeezed his hand back. "Sure, I guess that's fine. I'm off duty Saturday and Sunday. Although I do have a few…uh, chores to take care of. Late Saturday afternoon should work." She paused. "I really do appreciate your helping me through this, Doc…uh, Art." They both stood up, and she gave him a gentle hug. "Thanks again for your understanding and support."

He smiled and placed one arm gently around her shoulders as they walked out. Then Megan left to finish rounding on her patients without ever mentioning that her weekend "chores" included continuing her review of patient records that she had undertaken to try and validate Kacie's concerns.

# CHAPTER FORTY-FOUR

As Art Kinkaid had suggested, he and Megan made a return visit to Aldo's Italian Trattoria, this time on Saturday afternoon for a late lunch since neither of them had hospital duty. He picked her up at her apartment complex and they drove together.

It was a laid-back meal. She suggested a couple of her favorite dishes and her favorite red wine. He enthusiastically complimented her on all her recommendations.

Fortunately, conversation was equally easygoing, both veering away from anything hospital-related. Most importantly, neither Kacie nor the medical records situation were topics of discussion, a huge relief for Megan. She didn't want to dredge up her mixed feelings of sadness and anger at her friend's terrible fate. And she certainly didn't want Kinkaid to know how she was poring through hospital patient records for some explanation of what was going on.

When they finally left, it was early evening and they drove straight to her apartment complex, continuing their conversation for a short period while seated in his car. When ready to leave, he escorted her to the building's main entrance, where they stopped and she thanked him for an enjoyable afternoon. Before leaving, he reached out and held her in a warm hug, then gave her a firm kiss on her cheek.

Feeling a familiar stirring inside, she reached up with her hands pulling him closer and reciprocated with a more forceful, passionate kiss on his lips.

"How about coming up for a nightcap? I have several Italian varieties."

He hesitated briefly before responding, their eyes intensely locked on each other. "Sounds wonderful."

Megan smiled, grabbed one of his hands and led him up to her apartment, where they settled down on the sofa, sipping their drinks—until she leaned over, kissed him passionately once again, then led him to her bedroom.

# CHAPTER FORTY-FIVE

Sunday morning arrived too quickly. Megan's eyes opened slowly, only to find Kinkaid still asleep. She leaned over and gently kissed his shoulder.

He shuddered briefly, then opened his eyes. "Good morning."

Megan sat up, pulling the sheet around her. "Did you sleep well?" He smiled. "Sure did, although sleeping wasn't the best part of the evening."

She laughed. "I agree. Why don't you go shower and I'll make us some breakfast?"

"I'm not turning that down."

She swung her legs off the bed to stand, pulled on a robe, and directed him to the shower. "Breakfast will be ready in a jiffy."

Finished with his shower and dressed, Kinkaid ambled into the kitchen where Megan had prepared generous servings of bacon and eggs with home fries, toast, and hot black coffee.

They sat and finished the hearty meal with very little discussion until Megan spoke. "Thanks for the dinner yesterday. Actually, it was a very enjoyable day all around—especially last night.

Kinkaid smiled. "You're welcome. And I agree about the rest of the day and evening. It could actually become a habit."

Megan laughed. "Hold on there, pardner. Gotta take this slow."

He grinned. "Yeah, yeah. I know."

After one last cup of coffee, he gave her a goodbye hug and kiss, then left.

She went back to her bedroom and laid down for a while, lost in thought about the potential for a lasting and intimate relationship with Kinkaid, something she desperately yearned for.

It didn't take long, though, before her thoughts reverted to what she had planned for the day, and what secrets she might find when she dug into additional patient records. Resisting the urge to roll over and go back to sleep, she got up, showered and dressed casually for the day. Sitting at her desk with her laptop, she used a software program all hospital physicians were allotted in order to access their patients' records remotely as needed with their EMR credentials, and she began her review.

After several hours and several more cups of coffee, Megan had reviewed a large number of records, although she didn't keep count. She was more concerned with what she found, which was consistent throughout. Most importantly, it validated everything Kacie had been saying about the information in the records. And now, all the patients she herself had treated were included. "*What the hell?*" she blurted out loud. All the records, including hers and Kacie's, as well as those of other physicians, had several issues in common.

All the orders, notes, and final diagnoses were entered into the record under the treating physician's EMR credentials. Next, a specific genetic test was ordered for all patients. Megan obviously knew this was appropriate for certain patients when indicated by their medical history, family history or current condition. Ordering such an expensive test for all patients, however, regardless of indication or relevance to the patient's condition—wasn't considered good medicine nor cost-efficient.

But the one finding Megan was most curious about was the difference between the final diagnosis and the lack of support for it in the attending physician's notes for all the patient records she reviewed. Without exception, the final diagnosis recorded suggested a significantly higher level of complexity or severity of the patients' condition than what could be explained from the physicians' notes. *Why would that be?* After all, standard practice dictates that the patient's final diagnosis depends upon the history, physical examination findings, and laboratory results recorded in the patient's chart by the treating physician, which in turn determines the complexity and severity of the patient's condition. In other words, in all the cases Megan reviewed, the physicians' notes suggested one level of severity of illness, while the final diagnosis recorded was always consistent with a much higher level of severity. Now she was confused. Sure, an occasional instance of such a mismatch could be explained by physician error. But this was happening consistently on all patients and for all physicians, not just a select few. And the final diagnosis recorded always, without exception, reflected a severity of illness significantly higher, never lower, than what could be explained by the physician's documented history, physical exam and results of any diagnostic testing ordered. The more she thought about it however, something rang a bell.

Megan was familiar with the ICD—the International Classification of Disease—which assigns ICD codes for each disease. Every final diagnosis and associated tests and procedures have specific ICD codes, and of course each code has a certain level of reimbursement from government and commercial healthcare payors associated with the services provided.

Simply speaking, the more severe diagnoses and complicated procedures receive ICD codes which reflect that higher level of complexity and severity, resulting in higher levels of reimbursement.

As a physician employed by the hospital, Megan's main concern, and that of her colleagues, was the proper diagnosis and treatment of the patient, and ensuring their documentation supported that goal. Financial issues were not a main consideration.

As such, she, and likely all the physicians in her position, were not adept at actually coding the services they provide. That was left to coding experts in the finance department based upon the information provided by the treating physician in each patient's medical record.

Shaking her head, Megan didn't want to believe what she was thinking. *What if diagnoses were being changed to ones with ICD codes that suggest a level of complexity or severity not intended by the treating physician, but have higher levels of reimbursement—a practice referred to as upcoding? But why would physicians provide a final diagnosis to support upcoding for a given patient's care—essentially a fraudulent act—with no financial benefit to them?* She couldn't think of any explanation why they would. *After all, they were being paid a fixed salary by the hospital, and their main concern was appropriately treating the patient.* Which could only mean their diagnoses were being changed, and upcoded, by someone else and attributed to the physician. And she knew this for a fact, since she was now seeing this occur with her own patients for the first time.

*And what about the genetic testing issue?* She doubted all the patients in the hospital met the legitimate indications for the expensive test even though they all had it performed, which was just as insidious as the diagnosis upcoding occurring throughout the hospital.

She wanted to believe this was all random, the result of an inefficient system run amok as the result of inept leadership since Alan Fresney was fired.

Except this had billing fraud written all over it, and the evidence was overwhelming.

*This needs to be shared with someone I can trust. And I think I know who that might be.*

# CHAPTER FORTY-SIX

It was 6:00 p.m. and Megan was exhausted at the end of a long Monday. She was already tired when the day started from the marathon patient record reviews she completed the day before, and the shocking details of what she had learned. She was the hospitalist on call to the ER once again, and had admitted several new patients, as well as attending to the inpatients already on her service. Fortunately, her shift was ending soon and another hospitalist would assume the evening ER call duty and cover the patients she'd admitted. Megan briefly stopped by the Human Resources office to retrieve some information on a former employee that she had requested beforehand when her cell pinged and she looked at the text message.

*"Damn! It's the ER again and my replacement hasn't arrived yet. Will I ever get outta here?"*

She headed down to the ER to learn that the emergency was a high school football player that had severely fractured his leg. The orthopedist was on his way in, but the nurse needed an order for pain medication.

When Megan arrived in the ER, she immediately identified the patient, a strapping young male moaning and writhing in pain on a stretcher. She preceded her examination by introducing herself, a detail he had no interest in. All he wanted was something for pain.

The most revealing part of her exam was a grisly distortion of his lower left leg, the lightest touch of which elicited a loud groaning reaction. His body habitus was that of a muscular, athletically fit adult. In other words, a football lineman.

After she completed a cursory examination of the patient to affirm a good pulse in the affected leg, she sat at a computer station to access his record in the EMR, review his vital signs, and record her exam findings pending the orthopedist's more detailed exam. After she confirmed no allergies, Megan then calculated the appropriate dose of morphine for the boy's age and measured weight using the EMR medication ordering module, and recorded the order in the patient's record.

She then called the nurse over, a thirtyish male nurse she had never seen before, to alert him of her order.

"Are you new here, Arthur?" she asked, garnering his name from his ID badge.

"Yes, Ma'am. I'm an agency nurse."

Megan was slightly taken aback by how he addressed her—instead of using the standard medical prefix "doctor"—and confirmed his agency status by noting said designation on his ID badge.

Megan wasn't surprised, as the nursing staff shortage and the administration's use of agency nurses to supplement hospital employees was well known.

"I've placed an order for 10 milligrams oral morphine in his EMR chart," she advised the nurse to confirm the order with him. "That should hold him until the orthopedist arrives. If you need anything further, I'll be signing off to my night shift replacement when he arrives."

Megan returned to the patient and placed her hand gently on his shoulder, his game pads still in place. "We're getting you some pain medicine that might make you a little groggy. The orthopedic doctor will be here shortly."

The boy opened his eyes and mouthed a barely audible, "Thanks."

As Megan left, she called her incoming replacement and filled him in on the boy in the ER, signed out and drove home for some much-needed rest.

Back in the ER, the agency nurse named Arthur sat down at the computer terminal and logged into the same patient's EMR record with credentials that had been provided to him—but were not in his name. Once he finished typing in the medication order module, he administered the medication to the boy and texted a number in his cell before completing his shift for the day.

# CHAPTER FORTY-SEVEN

Exhausted, Megan went directly home and to bed without dinner after treating the boy with the fractured leg in the ER. When she awoke early the following morning after a solid eleven hours of sleep, she took a long hot shower before dressing, treated herself to a hearty breakfast and felt rejuvenated. She was still uncertain exactly what to make of the medical records issue that was now more concerning than ever after her extensive review of random records, and most importantly, with whom to share it.

Once at the hospital, she signed herself in to the employee portal and stopped by the hospital personnel department. From there she went to the ER to see how the boy fared after being seen by the orthopedist. But he wasn't there, nor had he been discharged.

"He's in intensive care," said the nurse manager when queried. "He had some significant breathing problems after receiving his pain medication and the orthopod casted his leg."

"Breathing problems? Seriously?" Megan was surprised. "I didn't see any allergies in his medical record, and the morphine was appropriately dosed for his age and weight."

The nurse shrugged. "Who knows? Probably just scared stiff and worked up over the injury curtailing his playing availability for a good while. He'll likely have that cast for months and need rehab afterwards. That's sure to put a crimp in his hopes for an athletic scholarship to college."

Megan started walking away. "Bummer. Thanks for the heads up. I'll go check on him."

When Megan got to the ICU, the boy with the leg fracture had been moved to the step-down unit, which was good news. He was sitting up, on mask oxygen, but comfortably breathing without assistance.

Megan introduced herself, but his memory of her in the ER was vague at best. She noted his sullen expression related to his leg injury, and tried to cheer him up with encouraging comments about a full recovery and function in due time, albeit with aggressive rehab, but his gloomy demeanor remained unchanged.

Forcing a genial smile, she patted him gently on his shoulder and said she'd try to make it back to see him before discharge. Then she left to continue her patient rounds.

That's when her phone pinged with a text message from Penny Salicio: *Urgent. Ty Prendersen wants to meet with you as soon as possible.*

# CHAPTER FORTY-EIGHT

When Megan arrived at the executive suite, Prendersen's office door was closed. Penny immediately phoned her arrival in to him, then disconnected. She stood and escorted Megan to the door. Before opening it, she turned to Megan. "You didn't hear it from me, but he's in a nasty mood."

Megan shrugged. "Thanks for the heads up," and entered as Penny closed the door.

Prendersen was sitting behind his desk looking at his computer screen. He motioned to the chair across the desk from him without looking at her. "Have a seat."

She sat down as requested. When he turned to look at her, the scowl on his face was intimidating. *Penny wasn't kidding about his mood!*

Prendersen didn't proffer a greeting, and instead got right to the point. "I just received some disturbing information from our IT department, Doctor. It appears you've been accessing a large number of patient records on a number of occasions as of late. Do you mind telling me what you're looking for? And before you answer, most of the patients are not on your service."

Megan shifted uncomfortably. *I can't believe he's tracking me!*

Caught off guard, she considered her answer. "Well, I have assumed the care of all the patients that were on Kacie Brendt's service, and I've needed to get up to speed on their issues and document my care, if that's what you're talking about. I guess they technically haven't yet been moved onto my service in the system."

He shook his head. "Actually, that's not what I'm talking about at all. Reviewing the records of Dr. Brendt's patients that you have assumed is reasonable. But the rest, the largest group, are all random patients. Since you don't have a medical reason to be reviewing their records, your actions could be construed as a violation of patient confidentiality. Perhaps you're not aware this puts the entire hospital at risk for losing required accreditation by regulatory agencies for failure to maintain processes to prevent such a violation of patient rights.

He leaned in closer to her. "And I can assure you. Doctor, that is not something we will allow to occur. As chief operating officer, I'll be advising the hospital president of your actions and ensure this conversation is documented in your employment record. Furthermore, it goes without saying that you should cease any further review of patient records in such a random manner unless it is specifically for medical care purposes."

Megan was flabbergasted and didn't know what to say, thinking it best not to divulge what she was really looking for— and found—confirming Kacie's repeated complaints about discrepancies in final diagnosis and random genetic testing without an indication in numerous patient records well beyond her own patients. Given that Kacie was never provided a valid explanation for those discrepancies by Prendersen, or anyone else in hospital administration, and what Megan confirmed in her review so far, she was convinced it was highly unlikely patient confidentiality was his true concern.

He stood, walked over to the door, and opened it. "You may leave now."

Megan walked out looking straight ahead without acknowledging Prendersen or anything he just said. As she left the suite and passed Penny without saying a word, Megan resolved to continue her search to validate Kacie's concerns.

*This needs to be sorted out once and for all. I owe that much to Kacie.*

# CHAPTER FORTY-NINE

After Megan left the executive office suite, she proceeded to round on her patients, still fuming from her encounter with Ty Prendersen. Her first instinct was to continue reviewing patient records to strengthen her case that something was awry with the documentation, as Kacie had suspected. She immediately felt a recurring pang of sadness for the loss of her friend.

Just then, her cell pinged. It was a text from Kinkaid: *Lunch? I'm heading to the cafeteria now.*

Megan responded with one word. *Sure.*

Her thoughts immediately went to their recent dinner together and the remainder of the evening. Her feeling of physical attraction to him was even stronger now. *Could this relationship be nurtured into a lasting and meaningful one?* It was something Megan desperately yearned for.

When she arrived at the cafeteria, she immediately saw him sitting in a window seat across the room. She wasn't very hungry, so she quickly grabbed a bowl of soup, walked over to the table and sat across from him. "Hey, thanks for the invite."

He smiled. "My pleasure." He swallowed a bite of his sandwich. "Actually, I really was hoping to catch you sometime today anyway just to let you know I really enjoyed our dinner date the other night, as well as the remainder of the evening. How about you?"

She countered with a coy smile. "Mm-hmm. Sure did."

"Great. That's what I was hoping," he said. "Then we can do it again sometime soon?"

Megan leaned forward. "You're on, Doctor. I'm looking forward to it."

He quietly chuckled. "Listen to us. We sound like two high school kids after the Saturday night dance!"

She nodded and grinned. "Yeah, feels good."

"Let's set it up, then. soon." He stood up. "I gotta get going."

She leaned forward. "Wait, I need to tell you something."

"Okay, if it won't take too long."

"It won't." She went on to describe Prendersen's meeting with her, including his assertion he would document her violation of patient confidentiality in her employment file.

Kinkaid appeared genuinely displeased. "That's absurd. It's not even within his purview to take such an action with a physician. He should have referred that to me if he had such a concern."

"That's what I thought too, which is why I'm telling you."

"Hmm. Tell me, what were you doing reviewing all those records anyway?"

She hesitated. "I've been wondering ever since Kacie commit …uh, died, what her allegation of patient record alteration was all about, or if it was even valid at all."

"And?"

"I was able to validate her concerns about final diagnoses not being compatible with the treating doc's documented findings for her patients and many others, including mine.

"I see. Anything else about the records?"

Megan was about to mention the diagnosis and upcoding issue but thought better of it, not wanting to sound like an alarmist. "Just some testing orders not relevant to the patient's condition, which was almost universal for all the charts I reviewed."

"So, in other words, nothing really different than what Kacie had been saying, correct?"

"Uh-uh."

"Then don't worry about it. I'll speak with Prendersen and get those comments about violating patient confidentially—which are ridiculous anyway—expunged from your file. Besides, any such action is the responsibility of the medical director, not a chief operating officer. He should stick to operations. And at that, I really do have to go. I'll give you a call to set up our next dinner date."

"Great. I'm really looking forward to it. She winked. "And after dinner as well,"

He chuckled as they walked out together but went their separate ways.

# CHAPTER FIFTY

Following her lunch meeting with Kinkaid, Megan finished her patient rounds for the day, including a new patient to admit, then stopped by the ICU to see how the football player was doing. She was pleased to learn he'd been discharged home with his leg casted and was otherwise doing well.

She left for home, intending to resume her review of patient records in the EMR remotely for the duration of what was left of the day and evening. Although somewhat hesitant after her meeting with Prendersen, her concerns were allayed by Kinkaid's reassurance he would talk with him and have his overreaching comments about her so-called violation of patient confidentially completely removed from her employment record. Despite other obstacles, real or perceived, understanding in more detail what was going on with the records had become more important to Megan than ever.

When she got to her apartment, she immediately stripped off her clothes and took a luxurious hot shower, toweled off and donned a pair of loose sweats. After eating some leftover sushi, she sat at her desk with a glass of wine and began reviewing additional patient records.

It wasn't long before her eyelids started feeling heavy, and concentrating on the computer screen was becoming more difficult. Besides, of the charts she reviewed, the pattern was unchanged—final diagnoses that were not supported by the physician's documented findings but were coded at a higher level.

And the practice of ordering genetic testing, rarely with a documented indication, also persisted throughout.

Just as she started dozing off, her cell rang. *Damn, that better not be the hospital.* After several rings, she realized ignoring the call was futile and she answered, hopeful she wouldn't have to return. "Hello."

"I'm trying to reach a Doctor Megan McLoren."

"Well, then, you've succeeded."

"I'm, uh, sorry for the lateness of my call and if I've awakened you..."

Megan sensed discomfort in his speech, and tried to allay his apparent uneasiness. "No problem at all. What can I do for you?"

"My name is Dr. Saul Denier. I'm the assistant medical examiner for the county.

Megan's ears perked up. "Go on."

"Yes, yes, of course. I performed the postmortem examination on Dr. Kacie Brendt, and I—"

"Excuse me, but how did you get my name and number?" Megan's eyes widened as she sat up straight, nearly spilling her wine.

"Yeah, right. I called the hospital and was transferred to a secretary, a Penny something or other and—"

"Salicio, Penny Salicio," interrupted Megan, somewhat irritated. "She's the assistant to the hospital CEO and medical director."

"Right. Well, when I asked for a next of kin contact, she said she didn't have any on record and went on to say you were quite close with Dr. Brendt. So, I requested your contact information and well, she obviously obliged."

"Okay, okay. What can I do for you?"

Denier hesitated. "As you may know, the police have concluded that Doctor Brendt's death was self-inflicted from a drug overdose."

Megan felt a tightness in her chest. "Yes, So I've heard, from a Detective Backstrom."

He cleared his throat before continuing. "Well, that's not exactly accurate."

Megan's chest tightness was worsening and she felt a knot in her stomach. "How so?"

"I'm sorry, but this is a little complicated. Dr. Brendt did have barbiturates in her blood, but also a large amount of undigested drug in her stomach, suggesting she died before all the drug could be absorbed into her bloodstream."

Megan had a puzzled look and shook her head. "I don't understand. How is that still not suicide?"

She heard him sigh before responding. "She also had a lethal amount of Fentanyl in her blood."

"Fentanyl? I assumed she would have obtained the barbiturates from the hospital. But any Fentanyl at the hospital is mostly used in the OR by an anesthesiologist and is for intravenous use, not oral."

"That's just it. She had needle marks in each arm consistent with Fentanyl injection. However, based on my analysis of the stomach contents, including the condition of the residual barbiturates there and the condition of hematomas at the injection sites, I concluded the IV Fentanyl had to be administered well after ingestion of the barbiturates."

Megan was confused. "What difference does it make, dammit? Either could have been fatal."

"I know this is difficult for you, Doctor, but actually, there is a difference. You see, the level of barbiturates in her bloodstream was not high enough to be fatal, but enough to make her extremely drowsy, meaning the Fentanyl would be the primary cause of death. Using the condition of the partially digested stomach contents to determine roughly the timing of barbiturate ingestion with respect to consciousness, I concluded it would have been virtually impossible for her to have self-injected the Fentanyl, since she would have been unconscious from the barbiturates. Which means—"

Megan stiffened. "Someone else injected the Fentanyl?"

"Yes, that's my conclusion."

"But then her death could no longer be considered suicide, right?"

"Correct. Based on the findings I described, I would consider her death a homicide."

"So, why didn't you write it up as such rather than suicide?"

"I did. Which is why I'm reaching out to you.

Megan was shaking her head "Huh? I don't understand."

"My boss, the chief medical examiner, chose to override my conclusion and deemed it self-inflicted—suicide."

Megan was confused. "Why would he do that, Doctor?"

"I really have no idea. He simply referred to my scenario as unlikely. However, our secretary did tell me he received a phone call just before he changed the death certificate to officially indicate suicide as the cause."

Megan's back stiffened and she shifted the cellphone to her other ear. "Phone call? Who from? Do you think it had something to do with overriding your report?"

"Sorry, I don't know. Our secretary said the caller simply referred to having some personal business with him, although she heard my boss say something like "sure, I'll take care of it" before he ended the call.

"Hmm. Do the police know about this?"

"Not that I know of. And I certainly wasn't going to tell them the cause of death was changed to suicide by my boss, either. It would probably cost me my job."

"I understand. Anything else you can tell me?"

"Not really. Just wanted to let family know, although I guess you can do that for me."

"Not sure if I'll be able to get any contact information if it's not on file at the hospital. But I'll see what I can do. In any case, thanks for reaching out to me. Much appreciated."

When the call ended, Megan was trembling—and pondering whether to scream out loud or just cry.

Either way, once again she needed to figure out her next steps.

# CHAPTER FIFTY-ONE

Breathless, Elsbeth Sentini rolled away from Wendell Courte and off the bed. The Senator turned onto his side and propped up his head with one hand, elbow on the bed. "Now that was some welcome back greeting."

She chuckled and wrapped a robe around herself. "Always happy to see you, senator."

"Right." Courte got out of bed and began dressing. "How's the cardiology program coming along? Still busy?"

"Uh-huh. It's a cash cow with all those referrals from the community heart fairs—and a surgeon with a low threshold for surgical intervention. A brilliant move by Wernuk and his team."

"And that troublemaker radiologist? Any more problems?"

"Not since he's been gone."

"Gone? Where did he—"

"Never mind. That's on a need-to-know basis, and you don't need to know."

"Hmm. Thanks for your sensitivity to my political status."

She pulled off her robe, exchanging it for her clothes. "My pleasure, senator."

He finished dressing. "And that nosy doctor who was questioning patients' records? Is she still causing trouble?"

She hesitated. "No, not anymore."

"Dare I ask why?"

"Sorry, another need to know. Although I can say your phone call to the chief medical examiner certainly helped our cause."

Courte smiled. "Glad to be of service."

Sentini was combing her hair, which had become disheveled during their robust encounter. "Unfortunately, another young physician she befriended has apparently taken up her cause and is poking her nose into the medical records of patients she's not caring for. In fact, you may know of her. Megan" McLoren.

Courte's eyes widened. "THE" Megan McLoren? HHS Secretary Allisyn McLoren's niece?"

"One and the same. But she won't—"

"Hold it right there, Elsbeth. She'd better not become another one of your "need-to-know" solutions. You know what her aunt dealt with at the FDA, don't you? And how she quashed that gene therapy conspiracy? Messing with her niece will only get you on her wrong side. She'll be all over your ass in a hot minute, and become your worst nightmare. And I won't be able to help you out of that one."

Sentini smirked. "Then we'll just have to be more discrete with her. In fact, I think we may already have it covered."

He shook his head. "Just keep me out of it, okay?"

"Sure thing. But you must agree you've enjoyed the financial benefits up to now."

"Yeah, but jeopardizing my senatorial status will cost me even more, both financially and legally."

"Don't worry, senator. We'll keep you clean."

Then they left separately, per their routine.

# CHAPTER FIFTY-TWO

It took Megan a good while to get her head around what she learned from the assistant medical examiner about the nature of Kacie's death. It was difficult enough to accept her suicide. —But murdered?

She was sitting with her arms wrapped around herself, rocking back and forth, and shaking. *Who would do such a thing? And why?* Assuming Kacie had discovered the same issue of diagnosis upcoding in patient records that she had seen for herself, it would have to be someone who found out what she knew and felt threatened by the possibility that Kacie would disclose such illegal practices to the appropriate authorities.

Just then she realized how similar Kacie's story was to that of Agacia Cortez.

*Why the hell didn't I think of that sooner?*

Different hospitals, but the same issue of patient medical record irregularities exposed by two different physicians who both died from what were presumed to be suicides.

*Coincidence? Or was it more than that? Maybe even much more."* And if Kacie's death really wasn't suicide but was just *meant to appear so and was really a homicide . . .*

She shuddered to think of Agacia suffering a similar fate.

Megan needed to know more.

# CHAPTER FIFTY-THREE

After convincing herself that the deaths of Kacie and Agacia were not coincidental, Megan decided her next step was to see if there was any connection between Regnant and the hospital where Agacia worked, a small, independent, unaffiliated community hospital halfway between Baltimore and DC., appropriately named Midway General Hospital.

Sitting in front of her laptop, Megan's online search for Regnant quickly returned a link for REGNANT HEALTH SOLUTIONS, along with the tagline, 'Helping healthcare organizations maintain financial sustainability while delivering optimum care to the communities they serve.'

Megan rolled her eyes, and continued to peruse the 'About' section, which was mainly the history of the company. She was surprised to learn that the background of Regnant's founder and president, Oskar Wernuk, was in pharmaceutical sales, although he had some experience in hospital operations as well.

When she saw a tab labeled 'Healthcare Partners' on the site's menu, she clicked it, carefully scrolling through a long list of hospitals and other healthcare providers and facilities, including laboratories and medical supply outfits. Encountering a tab labeled 'Newest Partners,' a brief search confirmed her hospital, Wallberg General in Massachusetts, as the most recent addition. Then she returned to the partners list, and sure enough, Midway General, where Agacia had worked, was there.

Megan shuddered at how frighteningly similar Kacie's and Agacia's situations were.

*If Dr. Denier, the assistant medical examiner, was correct in his conclusion that Kacie's death was a homicide staged to appear as a suicide, then there was every reason to believe Agacia suffered the same fate— to prevent them from exposing what appeared to be a scheme at their respective hospitals to defraud healthcare payors, including the government, by overbilling for services provided using up-coding—or for services not even provided at all.*

She went back to the Regnant website and returned to the 'About' tab. She revisited the narrative a little more closely and found something new, a description of a number of other ancillary services that were provided by Regnant, and owned by the company as subsidiaries, such as medical laboratories, pharmacies and rehabilitation centers, among others, all of which generated additional revenue for the company. But the one that really caught her attention was "Regnant Genetic Testing." Megan knew that genetic testing is a high-cost procedure, typically reserved for patients with specific medical conditions. And she remembered Kacie complaining about all the patients she reviewed having genetic testing for no specific indication, something Megan confirmed when she did her own reviews.

She sighed and shook her head. *Another illicit source of revenue for the hospital—and Regnant itself via its genetic testing subsidiary.*

Megan felt her chest tighten and her breathing become labored as she briefly recalled Prendersen's bogus and abusive admonition about her "violation" of patient confidentiality by randomly reviewing their records. But her thoughts quickly reverted to Kacie and Agacia. *Could I be next?*

That's when she pulled a business card out of her pocket.

# CHAPTER FIFTY-FOUR

It was Friday afternoon and Detective Helen Backstrom was laboring over some week-ending paperwork at her desk in the local police precinct station when her phone rang.

"Is Detective Backstrom in?" asked the caller.

"You're in luck," said the detective. This is Backstrom."

"I need to speak with you."

The detective frowned. "I'm sorry, I didn't catch your name."

"I didn't mention it. I'm Megan McLoren. We spoke at the hospital. You gave me your card and told me to call if I have any other thoughts about Kacie Brendt."

"Oh, right. What can I do for you, Doctor?"

"When are you available to talk?"

"I can talk right now."

"No, in person."

"Okay. I can stop by the hospital and"

"No, not at the hospital either. There's a little coffee shop near my apartment building." She gave her the address. "Know where that is?"

"Sure. I'm familiar with the place. When?"

"How about tomorrow? I'm on call tonight, but my shift ends at seven in the morning. Say about eight or eight-thirty. Does that interfere with your weekend plans?"

"Nah, eight-thirty works fine. Sounds a little ominous, though. What's up?"

"It's a bit complicated. I'll explain it all tomorrow. Thanks for meeting with me, detective."

"Sure. See you in the morning."

And Megan disconnected.

Backstrom just sat there, scratching her head, and wondering what to expect.

# CHAPTER FIFTY-FIVE

Megan was sitting at the back of the coffee shop, sipping a large cup of black coffee, no sugar. She considered herself a coffee purist, if such a distinction even existed. All the lattes and their sort were, in her opinion, simply social status fads. Her only exception was cappuccino, the Italian drink made with espresso and steamed, foamy milk.

When Detective Backstrom entered, Megan immediately noticed and raised her arm, waving to get her attention.

Backstrom stopped at the counter and walked over to sit opposite Megan with her own coffee in hand as directed by the barista. "What's up, Doctor? You seemed a little anxious on the phone."

Megan leaned forward. "Yeah, it's about Kacie Brendt."

The detective sipped her coffee. "Go ahead. I'm listening."

"Her death wasn't suicide. She was murdered."

Backstrom shot up straight, almost spilling her coffee. "Where did you get that from?

"The assistant medical examiner, a Doctor Denier, who did the postmortem exam. He called me because the hospital didn't have any next of kin on file for her."

"Hmm. So how did he determine she was murdered?"

Megan described everything Denier had explained about the barbiturates and how he concluded Kacie had been murdered by injection of a fatal dose of Fentanyl that she couldn't have self-administered.

Backstrom folded her arms. "Well, that's quite an elaborate scientific explanation for her death. Why wasn't it on the death certificate?"

"It was, originally."

"What do you mean by that?"

"According to Denier, once his post was completed, he drafted his report, which stated her death was homicide from a lethal dose of fentanyl that was injected, but not by her, as he described. He then turned the final report over to his boss, the chief medical examiner, who changed the cause of death on the final certificate to suicide by barbiturate overdose, not mentioning the injected fentanyl."

"Did he give any reason for that?

"Not according to Denier. However, he did say the chief examiner received a phone call shortly before he made the change, but he doesn't know who the caller was or what was discussed."

"Hmm. Seems like you're trying to make the case the chief changed the final report in response to whatever was discussed with that caller."

"I'm not trying to make any case, detective, just giving you the facts. And the fact is, the chief medical examiner gets a phone call from someone, then immediately changes the official cause of death determined by the assistant examiner, who actually did the post exam. Sounds a little too coincidental to me."

"Any idea who the caller was?"

"Uh-uh. Denier said he had no idea, but didn't disclose the change, even to the police, because he was in fear of losing his job."

The detective was scratching her chin. "Interesting, to say the least. Unfortunately, we can't act on that information without his corroboration. You think he would be willing to put it in writing?"

"Don't know, but my best guess is no, unless he's legally required to do so."

"Then it seems I'll have to pay him a visit and advise him it's now officially part of a police investigation. One way or the other, his boss will figure out he told us anyway, even if we don't disclose him as the source. It'll be obvious once we start pumping the chief about who called him and why he changed the final cause of death."

"Good luck with that."

Backstrom started getting up to leave, stopping midway. "By the way, any idea who would want her dead?"

Megan hesitated, not wanting to jump to any conclusions without adequate proof.

"Not really, although I think it's highly probable it had something to do with her persistent complaints about the irregularities she found with multiple patient records in the EMR. That's the electronic medical record, where all patient information is stored. She was getting lots of pushback from hospital administration every time she brought it to their attention. But I don't know anything else for sure. I'll let you know if I learn more."

"I guess that's it, then." The detective stood to leave.

Megan joined her. "Hold on. I'll walk out with you."

Once outside, they shook hands and went in opposite directions.

Neither of them noticed the man across the street watching them leave together, and covertly taking several photos with his cellphone.

# CHAPTER FIFTY-SIX

Oskar Wernuk was sitting in his office with Ty Prendersen and Elsbeth Sentini. They were meeting with the man they called their associate or simply 'the fixer.'

"So, what do you have for us?" asked Prendersen.

The fixer leaned back in his chair, reached into his pocket to remove a photo, and passed it over to Prendersen. "This was two days ago."

Prendersen took a long look at it, then passed it around to the others, each doing the same in turn.

The fixer elaborated on the photo. "It's your lady doctor and a police detective leaving a coffee shop, where they met for an hour or so."

Sentini scowled. "A police detective?"

The fixer nodded. "Uh-huh. The same detective who investigated Kacie Brendt's death."

"What the hell are they doing together?" blurted out Wernuk.

"It seems the assistant medical examiner called McLoren and let her in on the cause of death switch, and she wanted to share it with the detective."

"How do you know that?"

The fixer smirked. "The bug I put under a table, and the barista's willingness to make sure they were both seated at that table together—that is, once I mentioned I saw her pocketing customers' change and I knew the store manager."

Sentini smirked and shook her head. "Courte is not going to be happy to hear that McLoren told the detective about the medical examiner. The senator was supposed to stay clean in all of this."

The fixer shrugged. "No biggie. Just don't tell him about it.

"Really? That simple, huh?" Sentini's brows furrowed, her face and neck reddened. "Damn! It better not become public he made that call to the chief medical examiner or there'll be hell to pay. He's certainly not going to take the heat for that favor."

The fixer smirked. "Yeah, well, he'll just have to deal with it."

Sentini frowned and rolled her eyes.

"One more issue," said Prendersen. "McLoren has been quite busy looking into patient records herself, like Brendt was doing. No telling if she's going to put it all together, but I wouldn't be surprised, especially now that she has the detective involved. . . . "And on top of that, we've been tracking her online activity at home. Besides the patient records, she's spent a good amount of time on the Regnant website."

"What?" huffed Wernuk. "What's that about?

Prendersen shrugged. "Not sure, but my guess is to see if there're any similarities with other hospitals we've partnered with, and—"

Sentini scowled. "Okay, enough of this. What about the contingency plan we discussed?"

The fixer sat up straight. "Already in motion. Just waiting for you all to pull the trigger."

Sentini stood up. "In that case, it's time to act . . . ASAP, before she figures it out and shares what she knows with that detective. Then we'll all be screwed." She looked over to Prendersen. "Make the call and set up the meeting." And she stormed out, slamming the door behind her.

# CHAPTER FIFTY-SEVEN

It was Friday afternoon and Detective Hal Conyers was sitting at his desk in the precinct building not far from the city's Inner Harbor. He was immersed in his least favorite activity—paperwork. He left his desk, walked over to get himself a cup of coffee and sat back down. He took one sip and almost spit it out. *Should've known. Left over from the morning shift.* He walked over to the sink, and tossed the residual coffee down the drain then grabbed a Coke from the nearby refrigerator.

He sat back down at his desk and took one long swig of Coke. That's when his cellphone rang. He looked at the screen and saw the caller was Megan.

"Well, hello, Dr. McLoren."

"It's Megan, Detective. Remember?"

"Sure do, although you seem to have forgotten it's Hal here." They both chuckled.

"What can I do for you, Megan?" he said in a more serious tone of voice.

She sighed. "I have some disturbing information that may be relevant to the death of Agacia Cortez."

Conyers was about to take a sip of his soda but instead sat up straight and put down the can. "Go on."

"We've had what appeared to be a physician suicide by drug overdose here with precipitating factors similar to what led up to Agacia's death."

"How so?"

Megan shared the whole saga of Kacie's scrutiny of patient records in the EMR after she noted some irregularities and her anxiety and frustration when she couldn't get any support from hospital administration to resolve the issue. Then she described Kacie's subsequent death, which was initially deemed a suicide, precipitated by her anxiety and depression.

"Interesting," said Conyers. "Sounds eerily like Agacia's story."

"Uh-huh. And there are even more similarities. For one thing, the irregularities in the medical records are almost identical. It's a little complicated, so I won't go into it now. Let's just say in both cases, it involved enhancing the hospitals' revenue."

"Now that may just be coincidental, Megan. Every business looks for ways to enhance revenue, and I wouldn't think a fiscally responsible hospital would be any different."

"That's just it, Hal. This is no coincidence. Shortly after I started working at Wallberg, management brought in a consulting firm called Regnant Heath Solutions. A guy named Oskar Wernuk is the founder and CEO of the company. I don't really know anything about him or the company itself, for that matter. But essentially, they help manage the operations of financially struggling hospitals so they become more fiscally sustainable. And here's the really interesting part. When I researched Regnant online, I discovered that the hospital where Agacia worked, Midway General, a small independent hospital south of Baltimore, is also their client."

"Now, that really is something to chew on," said Conyers "So, are you saying that the suicides of Agacia and your Kacie are both related to this Regnant?

"Yes and no."

"Huh? What do you mean by that?"

"Yes, I think Regnant is somehow involved in both their deaths. But I don't believe either was a suicide. From the time you first contacted me about Agacia, I didn't believe it was suicide. She was too strong emotionally and self-assured. I just couldn't buy into it. Kacie was the same. And this time I know for a fact it wasn't suicide."

"How can you possibly be sure of that?"

"Because the assistant medical examiner who did the autopsy told me so."

"What? Are you serious?" Conyers sounded shocked.

Megan took a deep breath followed by an audible sigh, loud enough for Conyers to hear. "Are you okay, Megan?"

"Yeah, I'm fine. I won't go into all the specifics of his examination that led him to his conclusion, but he determined that although her demise appeared to be from a self-inflicted barbiturate overdose, further examination convinced him the cause of death was a lethal injection of fentanyl that occurred after the barbiturate ingestion.

"Damn. That's a *Quincy*-like moment."

"It surprised me, too. But there's more to it. Although he submitted his post report as a homicide, the chief medical examiner changed the final report to indicate a self-inflicted barbiturate overdose."

"Changed it? Why the hell would he do that?"

"No idea. But the assistant ME said his boss made the change immediately after a mysterious phone call he received, and that's how the final report read —suicide."

"And this assistant ME has no idea who the caller was?"

"Correct. And there was no way he was going to debate the cause of death with his boss for fear he'd lose his job."

"So, what are you getting at, Megan?"

"Agacia's death was designated a suicide, even though I never bought the scenario she would intentionally jump out a window. She was very stable and too strong-willed. Now Kacie's death, ruled a homicide by the assistant ME, is switched to suicide in a mysterious turn of events. And each worked in a hospital that was partnered with the Regnant company. If you accept the premise that Agacia's death wasn't suicide or accidental, this is way more than a coincidence. I just have to figure out exactly what it is."

"Understood. Let me know what you uncover, Megan, and I'll see if we can connect the two. Just one thing. If this Regnant company is complicit in both these cases as you believe, you need to be really careful. No telling what they might do if you start poking around more than you already have."

When they ended the call, Conyers scratched his head, deep in thought. Based on what Megan had just shared with him, he now considered Agacia's death highly suspicious for foul play, not suicide, or accidental for that matter. Just how he would prove it was another story altogether.

# CHAPTER FIFTY-EIGHT

After the phone conversation with Hal Conyers, Megan completed her patient rounds and signed off to a colleague, since it was early Friday evening and she was off duty until Monday morning. Which meant she would have the entire weekend at home to think about her next steps. She had already decided to work closely with Detective Backstrom to learn more about what exactly was going on at the hospital and what Kacie's death had to do with it. But she needed to figure out exactly what that collaboration might entail.

Since she assumed Kacie's murder was related to her obsession with the irregularities in the EMR patient records she had found, Megan knew she would have to proceed carefully to uncover whatever malfeasance the hospital's leadership and the Regnant Health team had been perpetrating and were possibly willing to kill for.

Finishing the last of her patient notes, she was getting ready to leave when her cellphone pinged. She took it out of her pocket and looked at the screen. It was Penny Salicio. *Mandatory meeting tomorrow morning at eight in the executive suite. Don't be late.*

*What the hell?* Megan's first impulse was to pass by Penny's office on the way out to see what the meeting was about—especially since it was going to be on a Saturday morning—but quickly decided better of it. Instead, she opted to go home and try to get some rest. If she could just stop wondering what the mandatory meeting was all about.

# CHAPTER FIFTY-NINE

Megan arrived at the hospital executive suite at 7:45 the next morning. Penny Salicio was seated at her desk, already clacking away on her computer keyboard, but stopped when she looked up and saw Megan. Penny hit speed dial on her phone and almost immediately said, "Dr. McLoren is here." She paused to listen, then said, "Okay."

She hung up and looked at Megan. "You can go on in now, Doctor."

Instinctively, Megan walked toward the conference room door, but Penny stopped her. "No, the meeting is in Ms. Sentini's office."

Megan pulled up short and gave her a puzzled look.

Penny stood, walked over to Sentini's office door and opened it. "Sorry," she said in a hushed voice as Megan passed by her to enter the room. Then she closed the door and returned to her desk.

Megan momentarily froze when the door closed, struggling to suppress the fluttering sensation in the pit of her stomach that suddenly overcame her at what she saw.

Each sitting in one of a row of chairs were Elsbeth Sentini, Ty Prendersen and an older gentleman she didn't recognize. The only reassuring sight was that of Art Kinkaid.

Sentini motioned to the lone empty chair facing the assembled group. "Have a seat, Doctor McLoren. And thank you for meeting with us. I'm pretty certain the only one of us that you might not recognize, understandably so, is Oskar Wernuk, founder and CEO of Regnant Health Solutions."

Wernuk lifted himself into a half-standing position and offered a nod of acknowledgment in Megan's direction before sitting back down.

Sentini was sitting with her legs crossed, and leaned forward, her gaze intensely focused on Megan. "Let me explain why I requested this meeting. Mr. Prendersen has advised me of some very unusual activity on your part in our EMR. It seems you've been extensively viewing random patient records, very much like what Dr. Brendt was doing for some time before her unfortunate suicide."

Feeling a tightness in her chest, Megan's first impulse was to debunk the notion that Kacie committed suicide. But she decided it would be too provocative at this point, and instead remained silent.

Sentini leaned back in her chair "So, what were you looking for in these records?"

"As I explained to Mr. Prendersen, most of the records belonged to patients that Kacie was following, and since I was assuming their care, I needed to bring myself up to speed on their medical status."

Sentini nodded. "I see. That certainly makes sense. However, he noted you were reviewing the records of many other patients as well, patients who were not cared for by Dr. Brendt, or yourself for that matter. Is that accurate?"

"Yes."

"So, again, what were you were looking for?"

"I was trying to confirm, or repudiate, what she described and was concerned about, and had shared with Mr. Prendersen."

"And what was that?"

"Kacie noticed many patients with discrepancies between the physicians' documented findings and the final diagnosis recorded, as well as tests ordered that were not relevant to the stated diagnosis."

"And you told Mr. Prendersen this?"

"Yes. And in fact, Kacie had already brought this to his attention multiple times for a number of patients, concerned that such inaccuracies could potentially be harmful to patient care."

"And what did he do?"

"His only response was that it must have been a glitch in the computer system, and he would check into it. But nothing changed, and the discrepancies continued, according to Kacie. That's what I was looking for when reviewing all those other records. I wanted to see if this was continuing to occur."

"And what did you find?"

"Discrepancies were still present, at least in all the records I reviewed."

"And did you bring this up with Mr. Prendersen?"

"Yes, when he called me in about it."

"What did he say?"

"Nothing about the computer issue. He simply accused me of violating patient confidentiality, and he would note that in my employment file."

"And you don't think you were violating patient confidentiality, even though they were not your patients?"

"Of course not. Wrong diagnoses and inappropriate testing can lead to the wrong treatment, potentially causing harm to a patient, harm that could be avoided by having a treatment plan consistent with the physician's findings and accurate final diagnosis. And this problem needs to be rectified. To say it was violating patient confidentially is bogus, and I told him so."

"Did you mention this to anybody else?"

"Sure did. I told Dr. Kinkaid. He agreed, and said characterizing my actions as violating confidentiality was outright ridiculous, and he would tell Prendersen so, as well as having that citation expunged from my employment record."

Sentini looked over to Art Kinkaid "Is that accurate?"

Avoiding eye contact with Megan, Kinkaid simply nodded in the affirmative.

Sentini stroked her chin. "Hmm. I think you need to re-focus on your primary responsibility, Doctor, which is caring for patients. All this combing through patient charts looking for evidence to support Dr. Brendt's nebulous claims may be distracting you."

Megan frowned. "How so?"

Sentini leaned back and folded her arms. "Unfortunately, a concerning issue has been brought to my attention." She looked over to Kinkaid. "I understand you recently cared for a young man with an injured leg in the Emergency Room."

Megan cleared her throat, considering her answer. "Cared for is a bit of an exaggeration. He was a high school football player with a broken leg, waiting for the Orthopedist to arrive. The leg had been splinted, but the nurse was requesting an order for pain medication, which I provided for him after confirming no allergy or other contraindication. He was in a good amount of pain, but I didn't engage in any other treatment."

Sentini nodded. "I see. And did you discuss this with the nurse?"

"Of course. I placed the order in his EMR record, then told the nurse exactly what I ordered."

"Do you know the nurse's name?"

"Arthur, I believe, or something like it. But I don't recall his last name. I've never seen him before that. He was an agency nurse, not one of our staff nurses."

"Did he comment on your order?"

Megan's eyes hardened. "Exactly what are you getting at with this inquiry?"

Sentini glared at her. "The nurse filed an incident report with Doctor Kinkaid."

Megan was confused, and appeared puzzled. "Incident report? What about?"

"I'll have Dr. Kinkaid explain that."

Kinkaid briefly averted his gaze away from Megan and down to some papers he was holding, "He claims you ordered the wrong medication for the patient's pain."

Megan squinted and shook her head. "What? I have no idea what he's talking about. I calculated the appropriate dose of oral morphine for his age, weight, and pain level using the system's built-in algorithm, let the nurse know, and placed the order in the EMR."

"That's just it, said Kinkaid. You ordered hydromorphone, not morphine. And although the dose of ten milligrams was appropriate for morphine, hydromorphone, as you should know, is five to seven times more potent than morphine, which means the patient was significantly overdosed with a powerful opioid and he suffered near respiratory arrest, requiring a stay in the ICU for breathing support. Fortunately, he recovered without further incident."

"Of course, I know the difference between the two opioids." Megan replied indignantly. "As I said, the order was for morphine, not hydromorphone. Check the order in the patient's EMR record."

Kinkaid hesitated briefly. "I did, and it's clearly for hydromorphone, and—"

"No way," she blurted out with a raised voice. "There must be some mistake."

Kinkaid was slowly shaking his head and his lips were pursed before he spoke. "I'm afraid not, Megan. The order for hydromorphone is signed in under your EMR credentials. Unless you gave them to someone else."

"No, I would never do that. I signed in as always and ordered the morphine, as I've said. If the system recorded hydromorphone instead, either there's a glitch in the EMR, or someone who had my EMR credentials signed in after I ordered the morphine and changed my order."

"Do you have any idea who that might be?"

"Of course not. I keep my credentials private, as we've been instructed, to prevent someone with nefarious intentions from fraudulently accessing the system."

"And yet you're proposing that's exactly what happened?"

Megan was becoming irate at this grilling, especially since it was conducted by Kinkaid, and her tone of voice reflected it. "I'm not proposing anything! I told you, I signed into the system, properly ordered morphine—not hydromorphone—at the appropriate dose for the patient's age and weight, then advised the nurse of the order and to treat the patient's pain accordingly. Megan paused to cool down her temper and allay her exasperation at this entire charade. "Did you even bother to ask the nurse why he didn't question me about the EMR order, supposedly for hydromorphone, when I verbally advised him that I had specifically ordered morphine? Instead, he just went ahead and carried out an EMR order for hydromorphone, even though it conflicted with what I told him. He could have pointed out the discrepancy, but never mentioned it to me. Don't you think that's more than a little odd? Even a violation of nursing procedure to confirm a questionable medication order?"

Kinkaid ignored her question and instead looked over at Sentini before he continued. "There's more to the incident report, Megan."

"More? Like what?"

"The nurse claims you were very unprofessional, condescending and arrogant towards him, particularly once you learned he was an agency nurse."

Now Megan was fuming. "That's ridiculous. Nothing like that even remotely happened. You can ask the other nurses. I never have that attitude with them, and I sure didn't start with him, agency or not."

Sentini raised her hand, signaling her to stop. "That's enough Doctor McLoren!" It seems to me that combing through all these medical records in an attempt to corroborate Dr. Brendt's concerns has become an obsession for you. I'm certainly not a psychiatrist, but given your close friendship with her, it's understandable why you would want to validate her concerns in order to explain her unstable emotional state, which led to her untimely self-inflicted demise. Unfortunately, this event in the ER, both the medication dosage issue and your less than professional interaction with the ER nurse, is an example of how your preoccupation with these patient record reviews has distracted you from your primary duties as a physician. If allowed to continue, this could negatively affect the quality of care you provide, potentially resulting in a catastrophic patient event, something we cannot, and will not, stand by and allow to occur by you or anyone else."

Megan's heart was racing. She was furious about Sentini's mischaracterization of her actions in the ER, as well as the continued false portrayal of Kacie's death as suicide. But she was hesitant to dispute either. So, she remained silent.

"Here's how I've instructed Dr. Kinkaid to proceed," said Sentini. "This discussion will be placed in your employment file as an incident report. "You, Doctor McLoren, will cease any further activity even resembling a review of random patient charts for some nebulous form of irregular documentation. If you continue to pursue any such activity, or discuss what you think is a problem, with anyone outside the leadership of this hospital, you will be suspended and Doctor Kinkaid will provide this report, including the suspension, to the director of your upcoming research fellowship, and recommend they reconsider accepting you into their program."

Megan felt her heart racing. She almost leaped out of her chair, eyes wide and face reddened. "You can't do that! I—"

"Oh, no? Are you willing to risk your future career on that? As board chairperson and hospital president, I can, and I will. And I'm certain your fellowship director would in fact be very interested to learn of your aberrant behavior before welcoming you into their program. After all, as prestigious as it is, they certainly expect certain performance and behavioral standards of their fellows, which this episode, unfortunately, does not portend."

Megan was speechless. She looked over to Kinkaid, her now pleading eyes imploring him for support.

He shifted his gaze away from her, not uttering a word.

Sentini stood. "Dr. Kinkaid will escort you out so you can resume your patient care duties." She looked over at Kinkaid, waving her hand toward the door. "Doctor?"

Kinkaid slowly eased himself out of his chair and shuffled over to the door, head down.

Megan stood and walked over to him, stopped and turned to look at Sentini. "This doesn't end here, and you will regret this." She turned and walked out, noticing Penny Salicio was not at her desk.

When Kinkaid followed her out of Sentini's office, Megan turned, glaring at him in disdain. "What the hell? I thought we had a real—"

"Please, Megan. Let me explain.—"

"Let you explain? Seriously? How exactly do you justify such an ultimate act of betrayal?"

He sighed, shoulders slumped. "Everyone has skeletons in their closet, Megan. Mine is a malpractice situation at my prior position that went south, and resulted in a resident I was supervising taking the brunt of the blame in order for the insurance company to protect me as a hospital employee. It unfortunately led to a major episode of depression on the part of the resident, and it destroyed his career. The only way I got this job was to do Sentini's bidding whenever a dicey decision needed to be made, or she would blow the whistle on me for what was essentially collusion with the insurance company."

Megan gave a sarcastic, muted laugh. "And you can live with that bogus justification for what you just did in there? Threatening to destroy my career to save yours?"

"Come on, Megan. Nothing like that will actually happen, as long as you stop trying to find something wrong with the EMR and patient records, which didn't exist in the first place. Just keep your head down and take care of patients, and that report will never see the light of day. Not here and not with your fellowship director. I promise."

Megan shrugged. "And have her hold it over my head to ensure I do her bidding like you, or she'll pass it on? What is it about the patient records that's so secretive, anyway?"

"Come on, Megan. Let it go, okay? Just let it go, and you can move on with your fellowship like nothing ever happened."

Megan turned to leave. "Sure. Just like all this never happened."

Walking out, she looked back at him over her turned shoulder. "And don't bother calling me again—Ever!"

# CHAPTER SIXTY

After leaving the executive suite, Megan rounded on her patients. Since she was off duty the next day, she signed out their coverage to one of her colleagues until she returned on Monday. When finished, she hurried out to her car in employee parking, still fuming over what she had just experienced—not only for Sentini's sham diatribe, but even worse, the part Art Kinkaid played in the entire fiasco.

*What a fool I've been! To think he knew about this the entire time we were together!*

She drove home faster than her normal speed, ignoring the risk of being pulled over. She just couldn't get away from the hospital fast enough.

Once in her apartment, Megan immediately took a hot shower, pulled on a pair of sweats and helped herself to a healthy pour of her favorite red wine as she attempted to pull together, into one coherent narrative, everything she knew about what was going on at the hospital.

When finished several hours later, Megan slumped in her chair. Despite her physical and emotional exhaustion, she was satisfied the document she had created shed a bright light on the malfeasance perpetrated at Wallberg General, and presumably at Midway General as well. Megan's dilemma was how to approach exposing all of this— at two different institutions, no less, without inciting Elsbeth Sentini to make good on the threat to derail her fellowship in Boston.

"I need help, someone on the inside." she uttered aloud.

That's when she remembered her recent inquiry with the hospital's Human Resources Department and checked for the information she had stored in her cellphone.

*Why didn't I think of that sooner, dammit?*

# CHAPTER SIXTY-ONE

"Hello, who's calling?" Alan Fresney didn't recognize the caller number on his phone.

"Mr. Fresney?"

"Yes."

"This is Megan McLoren, one of the hospitalists at Wallberg General."

"Yes, I recall you, doctor. What can I do for you?"

"First, please call me Megan."

He chuckled. "Sure. As long as you address me as Alan."

"Deal. I hope you don't mind, but I obtained your number from the hospital's HR department. I was wondering if you could meet with me. I have some questions about the hospital."

Megan was reluctant to break the silence that followed her request.

"Questions? What kind of questions?"

"Actually, it's kind of complicated, and — "

"That's okay, Megan. I can wait until we meet."

She suggested the same coffee shop where she had met with Detective Backstrom, and since she was off duty until Monday, they agreed on the next day, Saturday morning at nine.

After they ended the call, Megan sat back, her mind racing, second guessing her decision to meet with Fresney the next day and how much further she wanted to be involved in this fiasco.

*Should I continue my search for evidence exposing this fraudulent scheme, and risk losing my fellowship if Sentini makes good on her threat* to *share her bogus incident report with the program director? Or even worse, suffer the same fate as Kacie and Agacia?* She sighed. *Perhaps I should just stay out of it and let Detective Backstrom take over from here. After all, she's law enforcement and I'm just a physician, about to put this place in my rearview mirror and get on with my life. Why antagonize someone like Sentini and jeopardize my career?*

Holding her head in her hands, she pondered her predicament. Then she had a sudden epiphany, recalling the courage and resilience Allisyn displayed as she confronted adversity at the FDA.

*No, I must see this through, if only to provide a measure of justice for Kacie and Agacia, as well as any patients who were avoidably harmed because of inadequate or incorrect treatment due to falsification of their medical records for the sole purpose of increasing hospital revenue.*

She poured herself another glass of wine and collapsed on her couch, thinking about how she would make sense of all this with Fresney the following day.

# CHAPTER SIXTY-TWO

The next morning, Megan arrived at the coffee shop an hour before the time she and Fresney agreed upon. She grabbed a coffee and a breakfast sandwich and sat at a table toward the rear of the room. Alternating sips of coffee with bites of her sandwich, she pulled an envelope from her pocket that contained two items. One was a printed copy of what she planned to share with Fresney. The other was a photo of the hospital's former president she had obtained online, since she wasn't sure she would recognize him.

When he entered, she waved him over and he took a seat at her table.

"Thank you for meeting with me, Mr. Fres—uh, Alan."

He smiled at her. "No problem. Megan, right?"

"Uh-huh."

He waved the barista over, and ordered himself a coffee and a refill for Megan.

When his coffee arrived, he took several sips before speaking. "So, you've really piqued my curiosity. What is it you want to discuss about the hospital?"

Megan took a deep breath. "First, let me say you've really been missed since leaving. Part of that is what we're going to discuss, but it's also due to the fact that the staff holds you in very high regard."

"Well, that's very kind of you to say, Megan."

She took a sip of coffee and handed him a sheet of paper with her written summary. "Rumor has it you, uh, left because of Regnant."

He smiled. "Sort of. I had some prior familiarity with that company and made it clear I was not in favor of bringing them in to work with us. Since it was Sentini's idea to partner with Regnant in the first place, that didn't sit well with her. So, as board chair, she strong-armed the other members into supporting her recommendation to let me go rather than risk my undermining the hospital's relationship with Regnant. And then, of course, she appointed herself as CEO." He paused while briefly scanning the notes she provided. "I'm guessing what you have to tell me has a good bit to do with Regnant's management."

"Mhmm. " She hesitated. "Have you remained in touch with anyone at the hospital?"

"Yeah, a few people I was particularly fond of."

"Anybody in the finance department?

"Uh, actually, Lyle Probey, CFO. Why do you ask?"

"Well, I was wondering if subsequent to leaving, you've heard anything unusual about the Regnant engagement."

"Unusual? You mean other than the typical staff grumbling about new policies and procedures, training and so on? Oh, and there's always complaints about learning to use a new EMR system. Docs are especially loathsome of having to learn a whole new system of documentation, medication and order writing, etcetera."

Megan nodded. "Have you specifically heard any concerns from the medical staff about documentation in the Regnant EMR?

He frowned. "I'm afraid I haven't had any contact with physicians since the unfortunate death of Mitch Harwick in that terrible accident."

Megan's eyes widened and she leaned forward. "Are you convinced that was an accident?"

"Of course. That driveway of his was a disaster waiting to happen, and the snow and ice that night was awful."

Megan shrugged. "I guess."

Fresney winced, appearing shocked. "You guess? Are you saying it wasn't an accident?"

"I'm not saying anything, just questioning. After all, from what I understand, he didn't make any friends with Sentini or Regnant management when he called out Trevor Quinne for performing unnecessary invasive cardiac procedures while the guy was bringing in big bucks for the hospital with those procedures."

"Hmm. Now you're sounding like a conspiracy theorist."

"I'm just saying. After all, his death wasn't too long after he brought up the Quinne issue."

Fresney's eyes narrowed. "Yeah, I'm sure Sentini and Wernuk weren't happy with Mitch's questioning Quinne's practice. But responsible for his death? I can't imagine they would go that far." He took a sip of coffee. "So, what's this physician documentation issue you referred to?"

Megan sat up straight. "Some physicians have noticed irregularities in their documentation."

He shot her a puzzled look. "Irregularities? What do you mean by that?"

"Things like altering a patient's diagnosis the treating physician originally put in the medical record and orders for some specific testing that the treating physician never requested."

"Huh. Sounds pretty serious. What did Wernuk say about that?"

"His head of operations, a guy named Prendersen, just brushed it off as glitches in the system that would be corrected. But it's still happening, and it may have financial implications, not to mention posing a risk to patients."

"Now that you mention all this stuff, there is one issue I know about from Probey. He said Wernuk has the billing department coding all physician visits and procedures routinely performed in the physician office building on campus as having been performed in the hospital."

Now Megan looked confused. "So what? They're part of the same organization, right?"

"Yes, but it's not quite that simple. Any service delivered in the hospital will always be reimbursed at a significantly higher level than if done in the office."

"So, you're saying they're intentionally falsifying the location of services provided in the physician's office as taking place in the hospital in order to receive higher reimbursement?"

"Exactly. And Probey's uncomfortable with it. He brought it up to Sentini, who simply blew him off, which isn't exactly a surprise, since she's known to have a healthy financial interest in Regnant, both herself and her senator friend actually, which is why she brought Wernuk to Wallberg in the first place."

"senator? What?—"

Fresney smirked. "Wendell Courte, Massachusetts senator. He and Sentini are in bed togetherliterally and businesswise. He's the one who pulled some strings with the state agencies regulating hospital operations and got them to quickly approve the hospital's request to revive its dormant interventional cardiology program."

Megan frowned. "Uh, isn't that a bit of a conflict of interest?"

Fresney smirked again. "Ya think? He's a politician, after all. What else would you expect?" He paused. "So, what are you going to do with this information?"

Megan was silent, staring off to the side and deep in thought about her recent meeting with Detective Backstrom.

"Megan, did you hear me? What are you going to do next?"

She slowly turned her head, her eyes meeting his. "Can't say for sure."

*But I do have a good idea.*

As they left and went their separate ways, Megan took out her phone and pressed a number on her speed dial list.

# CHAPTER SIXTY-THREE

Megan stood in a drizzle outside Union Train Station on Massachusetts Avenue in Northeast D.C., hailing a taxi. Always thrilled to spend time with Allisyn, she was ambivalent about this visit, given the nature of what she was about to share with her.

Besides being her familial aunt, Megan considered Allisyn her closest friend and confidant. Neither hesitated to share with the other the most personal aspects of their respective lives. So, when Megan unraveled the fraudulent and dangerous scheme put in place by Elsbeth Sentini and Oskar Wernuk on behalf of WGH and Regnant, she had no doubt Allisyn, as secretary of Health and Human Services, would want to know the details. And when Megan called her with a brief, thumbnail summary of what she had uncovered, she wasn't surprised when Allisyn suggested an immediate meeting at her D.C. office if Megan could get away from the hospital for a day or two. Fortunately, she had some unused vacation time and signed her patients off to a fellow hospitalist, not expecting this to be a long visit. Her train ride from Boston provided an opportunity to review her notes—the same summary she had given Fresney—and make sure she wasn't missing anything important.

By the time she arrived at the Department of Health and Human Services—HHS,—housed in the Humphrey Building on Independence Avenue in SW Washington, the light rain had tapered off. Exiting the taxi, she shook off the residual wetness on her clothes, regretting not having brought an umbrella. After a security check and sign-in at the lobby desk, she took the elevator to Allisyn's office on the second floor.

Ginger, Allisyn's trusted assistant at the FDA who followed her to HHS, gave Megan a warm welcome, then ushered her into the secretary's office, where Allisyn promptly rose from her desk chair, walked over and gave Megan an exuberant hug. "Good trip, I hope?"

Megan nodded. "Uh-huh. Just a little soggy."

When they broke their embrace, Megan immediately recognized the man sitting in an armchair across the room as Phil Martinez.

Allisyn and Martinez, an undercover FBI agent, first met when, as FDA commissioner, she confronted a biotech firm's conspiracy to defraud the agency. They were "a thing," as Megan often referred to their relationship, since then.

He stood up and greeted Megan with a friendly hug. "Great to see you again, Megan. And congrats on your fellowship."

Elsbeth Sentini's threat still on her mind, she hesitated briefly before responding with a muted "Thanks."

Allisyn walked over to them. "I hope you don't mind that I asked Phil to join us, Megs. From the little you've told me, I'm sure he'll be equally interested to hear the full story. Want some coffee?"

Megan shivered. "Sure. I'm a little chilled from the rain."

Allisyn buzzed out to Ginger and asked her to bring in three cups of coffee, black no sugar. Then all three sat in armchairs across from each other.

After the coffee arrived, Allisyn leaned back in her chair, arms folded. "Okay, Megs, ready to tell us the entire story?"

Megan nodded and gave them each a copy of her summary notes. "When I first arrived at Wallberg General, the hospital was apparently having major financial issues, so they brought in a consulting and hospital management firm, Regnant Health Solutions, led by one Oskar Wernuk, on the recommendation of

Elsbeth Sentini, chairperson of the hospital board and a highly influential attorney in town."

She then spoke of how a cardiac surgeon was recruited by Wernuk and community heart fairs formed to refer patients to him, resulting in a prodigious number of invasive cardiac procedures, often with minimal, if any, indications, followed by the suspicious death of the radiologist who called him out on it.

Next, she focused on Kacie Brendt's persistent concerns about the documentation issues in the EMR that were consistently discounted and blown off by management, culminating in her death that was reported as a self-inflicted drug overdose but was then debunked by the assistant medical examiner who considered it a homicide staged to appear as suicide.

Sipping her coffee with a slight tremor in the hand holding her cup, she spoke of her heartbreaking phone call from Hal Conyers, the Baltimore homicide detective all three of them knew so well, sharing the terrible news of Agacia Cortez's death by falling from a window—after she discovered and complained of similar patient record documentation issues at a small community hospital outside of Baltimore that was also working with Regnant. She started tearing up. "Although her death was reported as suicide, I knew Agacia like the back of my hand, and there's no way in hell she would ever consider jumping out a window even under the most difficult of circumstances. And her husband, Paul, agrees. It was staged to appear intentional just like Kacie's overdose, which means they were each murdered for what they had in common. Both unintentionally exposed Regnant's scam for what it is—healthcare fraud. Which undoubtedly is being replicated at every hospital partnered with Regnant."

She stopped and took a deep breath, then went on to explain how her own review of patient records corroborated the upcoding of patient diagnoses, resulting in greater reimbursement, even though it was the incorrect diagnosis. She also described the inappropriate use of an expensive genetic test for all patients, even when not indicated, that was being billed to the patient or the insurer, and that the laboratory performing the test in fact was owned by Regnant itself, a clear conflict of interest.

Then she explained what Fresney had shared about falsely coding physician visits and procedures performed in their offices as having instead taken place in the hospital, again generating higher reimbursement.

Megan closed by describing her confrontation with Sentini and Kinkaid, and their false allegation that she ordered the wrong medication for the injured football player in the ER and disrespected the nurse, threatening to derail her fellowship by providing the program director with a sham adverse event report.

Megan's dismay was evident, eyebrows furrowed and face reddened. "That's when I realized they suspected I was on to their billing scam, and this ER event was all a set-up to keep me from exposing it."

Summary sheet in hand, Martinez was shaking his head. "That's one hell of a story, Megan. So sorry your two friends got caught in the middle of this brazen scheme, one of the worst cases of healthcare fraud I've encountered. The financial impact must be enormous." Megan nodded. "Even worse is the needless loss of life. Agacia, Kacie, and others, as well as the harm to unsuspecting patients, when their correct diagnosis supported by the physician's documentation, was replaced with an incorrect, up-coded diagnosis to procure higher reimbursement, but often leading to delayed or inappropriate treatment, and patients with complications from an unnecessary, invasive procedure. And the young football player whose life was jeopardized to falsely discredit me. So much harm and most, if not all of it, avoidable."

Up until that point, Allisyn hadn't said a word. But the pained look on her face spoke volumes. "I'm sorry you've had to experience this, Megs, and especially for the loss of your friends. Healthcare fraud is a huge problem in this country, with an annual cost close to one hundred billion dollars. In fact, HHS, in conjunction with the DOJ and FBI, has a Healthcare Fraud Strike Force to interdict such activity. And Phil happens to be a special agent on that group. She turned to Phil. "What do you think?

"I'll be bringing this to the Strike Force for action as soon as possible." Megan sighed. "Thanks, Phil. The company's website has a list of all its client hospitals, including Midway General Hospital, a small independent hospital in a community between Baltimore and DC. where Agacia worked, and I think it's safe to assume they all have the same business model, including fraudulent billing and unnecessary tests and procedures. Once I found that out, I was certain her death wasn't self-inflicted either, but instead staged to look like it was, again, just like Kacie. And that's what I told Detective Conyers. Agacia's and Kacie's persistence must have posed a real threat to Regnant and both hospital's management that their scheme would be exposed for the fraud that it is. Fresney, the former CEO at Wallberg, said part of Wernuk's program is sharing some of the financial return accrued with whomever introduced his organization to the hospital in the first place. Like Sentini at Wallberg, who Fresney said has a financial interest in Regnant, along with her lover, a senator no less. A guy by the name of Courte, and—"

Allisyn shot up straight in her chair. "Wendell Courte?"

"Yeah, that's him. Why, you know him?"

"Huh, do I ever. He's the most condescending and obnoxious pain in the ass ever. He's always hounding me to come down hard on healthcare insurance companies for poor reimbursement to hospitals while their execs have bloated salaries, and hounding me to do something about it. I guess he found a better way, albeit illegal, by hooking up with this Sentini and Regnant."

Martinez nodded as he wrote some notes on the summary sheet Megan had provided. "I'll take all this back to the Strike Force and keep you informed when we make a move on your hospital."

Megan slouched in her chair. "Thanks. Now I just have to figure out how to handle Sentini's threat to derail my fellowship with her fabricated incident report on me. If that gets to the director, I've got problems."

Allisyn nodded in agreement. "I think I can help with that one. I'll be having a little talk with Senator Courte as soon as possible. And when he hears what his options are, I think he'll be having a talk of his own with his lady friend to quash that report."

Allisyn stood up, looking at her watch. "What time is your train back, Megs?"

"Seven. A little later than I wanted."

"Hmm. It might be a little tight, but what do you say the three of us get a quick bite, then get you over to Union Station?"

"Sounds good."

Allisyn looked over to Martinez. "You in, Phil?"

"You bet."

They took a cab to Old Ebbit Grill, a favorite of Allisyn and Martinez and many others over the years who worked in D.C. It was a casual meal, and when finished, they took a cab to Union Station, where they said their goodbyes and Megan boarded her train for the return trip to Boston, then back to Wallberg General, where she would await word of imminent action on the hospital's management and that of Regnant Health.

# CHAPTER SIXTY-FOUR

Two weeks after Megan returned from her visit with Allisyn and resumed her clinical duties, three black sedans pulled up to the front entrance of Wallberg General Hospital, and one man exited the first of the cars. After stopping at the front desk for directions, he made his way to the office of the hospital CEO. Displaying his credentials to Penny Salicio, he asked to speak with Elsbeth Sentini. Penny called Sentini in her office, announced the visitor and escorted him in, closing the door behind her as she left.

Holding an envelope, the man introduced himself as Special Agent Phil Martinez, unit leader of the FBI Healthcare Fraud Strike Force. "This is a federal warrant allowing a full examination of all the hospital's records, to include any and all patient records, written or electronic, as well as any documents pertaining to the hospital's billing and financial activities, and to obtain digital or alternate copies of all said materials as determined necessary. The warrant also mandates free access to any hospital employee to be interviewed by an appointed federal agent without interference on the part of hospital management. Failure to abide by the terms of this warrant, including but not limited to concealment or destruction of any pertinent materials, is a federal offense and subject to punishment by law."

Martinez tossed the envelope on her desk, turned and left her office without another word.

Sentini was stunned. She picked up her phone and called Oskar Wernuk in his office. When he answered she immediately shared what just occurred.

There was a brief silence before he spoke. "I know. The Feds were just here."

————————

Outside, the three sedans were slowly emptied of their remaining passengers, both men and women, all smartly dressed in conservative business attire and identifying as FBI agents and members of the Healthcare Fraud Strike Force. The group consisted of legal experts, experts on healthcare documentation and billing, and computer specialists. All were trained and laser-focused on the current proliferation of fraudulent billing by providers of healthcare services, victimizing both government and commercial payors.

All this activity came as no surprise to Megan, since Phil Martinez had given her advance notification of the raid, exactly what the agents would be looking for, and were prepared to reach out to her as needed to corroborate the fraudulent manipulation of patient records by upcoding their diagnoses and ordering the genetic testing from Regnant's own lab without any order or indication by a physician, all done to illegally enhance hospital revenue.

Word of the raid spread rapidly throughout the hospital as the agents dispersed to multiple locations, with different versions from hospital staff of what was actually happening. The most frequently mentioned was some kind of drug bust, but that dwindled as the agents went into action.

The billing-oriented agents went directly to the Finance Department for evidence of the reported fraudulent practices, while the computer specialists were accessing all electronic files, focusing on patient records, digitally transcribing all such data onto portable hard drives for further evaluation and evidence of billing and other financial wrongdoing at the patient record level, with emphasis on upcoding and other fraudulent acts reported by Megan.

As all this activity transpired, two other similar raids were taking place—one at Midway General Hospital, where Agacia Cortez had worked, and the other at the office of Regnant Health Solutions, the latter to determine how widespread the fraudulent scheme actually was.

In the meantime, Megan decided to keep her head down, take care of her patients and look forward to starting her fellowship. The outcome would become evident soon enough.

*If I only knew the status of that damn bogus incident report Sentini threatened me with . . .*

# CHAPTER SIXTY-FIVE

The Strike Force raid on Wallberg General Hospital took nine hours and provided damning evidence of the fraudulent billing scheme perpetrated under the direction of Regnant Health with the willing participation of the hospital's management, led by Elsbeth Sentini.

The concurrent investigation at Midway General indicated the practice of fraudulent billing had been implemented there as well, while the other raid at Regnant's office confirmed multiple hospitals under their management. Preliminary investigation of that list revealed the same scam being perpetrated elsewhere.

As architect of this far-reaching healthcare fraudulent billing scheme that affected Medicare and Medicaid, as well as commercial healthcare insurers, Oskar Wernuk was indicted for conspiracy to defraud the federal government.

For her role in bringing Wernuk and Regnant to WGH in the first place, Elsbeth Sentini was indicted as a coconspirator. At Allisyn's request, Phil Martinez made sure Sentini never let her bogus incident report on Megan see the light of day or in any way reach Megan's fellowship director. He had no trouble convincing Sentini of the highly negative effect noncompliance with that requirement would have on her indictment proceedings for conspiracy to defraud, including probable disbarment.

By unanimous vote of the remaining board members, Sentini was dismissed as WGH chairperson, along with a lifetime ban on her participation on the board. Also, by unanimous vote, the board invited Alan Fresney to return as hospital CEO, which he accepted and immediately requested a quality review of Trevor Quinne's cardiac procedures by the state board of medicine. And he had no trouble convincing the hospital board members that Regnant's EMR system should be replaced with a nonproprietary, mainstream system that couldn't be misappropriated for illegal or otherwise questionable purposes.

Finally, at Megan's request, Martinez contacted Detective Backstrom, and together they initiated an investigation into the deaths of Mitch Harwick and Kacie Brendt, both suspected to be related to Regnant and the billing fraud conspiracy.

They were also to work concurrently with Hal Conyers in Baltimore to determine if there was a connection to Agacia Cortez's murder as well.

# CHAPTER SIXTY-SIX

Megan was taking a coffee break from rounding on her patients two days after the FBI raid when her phone rang. She looked at the screen for the caller ID and immediately felt an anxious tightening in her chest and dryness in her throat.

"Hello?" was all she could manage to say.

"Doctor McLoren? It's Helen Backstrom."

Megan hesitated, taking a deep breath. "What can I do for you, detective?

"Do you think we can meet to talk?

Megan's anxiety increased. "Have you caught up with Agent Martinez yet?"

"Yes, I have. And there are some developments I want to share with you."

"Tomorrow morning, for coffee?"

"Perfect. Same place, say around eight?

Now Megan was really anxious. "Works for me. See you then."

After they disconnected, Megan remained seated. pondering what it was the detective had to share with her. *Guess I'll just have to wait.* She finished seeing her patients and signed out, since she wasn't on call for the evening and was able to leave early. Still, as she drove home, she couldn't keep her mind from racing through all sorts of scenarios.

# CHAPTER SIXTY-SEVEN

The next morning, Megan arrived at the coffee shop early, at 7:30, surprised to find Backstrom already seated, coffee in hand, a second one, covered, on the table. She walked over and the detective slid the second cup over to Megan. "Black, no sugar, right?"

Megan smiled, and sat across the table. "Uh huh. thanks, detective."

Backstrom smiled back. "My pleasure, but one request. Please call me Helen."

Megan smiled. "Sure, as long as you reciprocate with Megan."

"Deal . . . Megan."

Megan was anxious to hear what Backstrom had to say. "So, what are these developments you referred to?

"Right. I received a call from Doctor Denier.—"

Megan shot up straight in her chair, almost spilling her coffee. "Saul Denier?"

"Yes, the assistant medical director."

"Does he have some new information about Kacie's death?"

Backstrom nodded. "When he did his post, he looked for evidence of assault besides the needle marks from the fentanyl injection. He was initially checking for a possible sexual assault, but nothing turned up. Then thinking she may have tried to fight off her assailant, he checked her hands, with particular attention to her fingernails—"

"And?"

"Sure enough, he found small pieces of skin that weren't hers under all her fingernails, indicating she must have really fought back and scratched the hell out of whoever it was. So, he ran a DNA test on all the skin he dug out, and had us see if we could get a match on any one of several crime databases, including the FBI's, but they all turned up negative. When I shared this with your FBI friend, Agent Martinez, he suggested doing the same with Interpol, and bingo, got a match right away. A guy by the name of Yuri Shivers, notorious throughout eastern Europe, with a rap sheet long enough to stretch from here to there."

Megan shrugged. "Yeah, but he's probably long gone now."

"That's what we thought too, but we got lucky. We got his picture from Interpol and put out a BOLO, and—"

Huh? BOLO?

Backstrom smiled. "Police speak for "Be On the Lookout" alert.

Megan chuckled. "That's a new one for me. So, what happened?

Part of the alert was to detain anyone remotely resembling his description or otherwise acting suspiciously, and issued a warrant to have any such suspect held and checked for a DNA match. If we get this guy, it's a big deal. His targets go way beyond Kacie and Harwicke, especially in Europe, where he's wanted for complicity in multiple murders and high-level assassinations, including government and political figures. If we can prove a connection with this Wernuk guy from Regnant, it's just as big a deal."

"Do you think he could be a suspect in Agacia Cortez's murder as well?"

"Most likely, f we confirm a connection with Wernuk. To that end, Martinez has notified a Detective Conyers in Baltimore."

Megan smiled. "Yes, I know him well."

Backstrom took a big sip of her coffee. Just then, her phone rang. She listened for a minute or so before turning her attention back to Megan. "That was Martinez. They just nabbed him at JFK, trying to leave the country. They did a rapid DNA test and bingo again, he's a match. The Feds are going to take it from here because of his history in Europe, and he'll probably be deported and taken into custody by Interpol agents. But he can still be charged with Kacie's murder by virtue of the DNA match."

Megan took a deep breath. "Thanks for all your work on this, detect… Helen."

She paused before finishing her coffee. Unfortunately, "I've got to get back to seeing patients."

Backstrom smiled. I'll let you know if anything comes of this guy, Megan "Let's stay in touch."

Both standing, Megan approached the detective and gave her a friendly embrace. "Definitely, Helen. And thanks for everything."

And then they left and went their separate ways.

# EPILOGUE

Megan stood in front of the large building in downtown Boston, home of the infectious disease fellowship and research program she was finally about to begin.

She stood there for several minutes. Although it had been a struggle, she finally was able to put thoughts of her time at Wallberg General behind her. She promised herself not to follow the media coverage that labeled the hospital a posterchild for healthcare fraud. But she couldn't avoid the periodic news snippets. She was hopeful Alan Fresney could right the ship and wished him luck. At least Elsbeth Sentini was gone, prosecuted for conspiracy to defraud the government and disbarred. Regnant Health was dismantled, its founder, Oskar Werner, was also prosecuted for conspiracy to commit healthcare fraud at Wallberg, but also for setting up multiple hospitals with the same fraudulent billing scheme, and then profiteering from their illicit revenue. Wendell Courte wasn't indicted, but he was sanctioned by the Senate for his complicity in the fraudulent activities of the hospital by way of his relationship with Sentini and his financial investment in Regnant. Art Kinkaid wasn't implicated in the manipulation of the hospital documents, but he resigned and dropped out of sight.

What Megan couldn't forget was the harm that befell so many individuals—patients who were not appropriately treated because their diagnosis was manipulated to improve hospital reimbursement, others who suffered complications from invasive procedures performed without appropriate indications, but for financial gain. And the boy with the leg injury in the ER, an innocent bystander of a diabolical scheme to discredit Megan herself.

But what brought tears to her eyes was the needless deaths of Kacie Brent and Agacia Cortez —both colleagues, friends, and victims of Regnant's and its partner hospital's greed and fear their billing fraud would be uncovered.

So much harm. So avoidable.

She gently wiped the tears from her eyes and looked up at the building, a faint smile on her lips.

*Finally, I can get on with my life.*

And she walked up the steps to the building's entrance.

>>>>>>>>>>>>>>>

# Author's Notes

Although Avoidable harm is a fictional story of my creation, the narrative sheds a light on two real-life issues plaguing today's healthcare environment:

The First is Healthcare Fraud, costing upwards of $100 billion annually. Learn more on the websites for the FBI and the Department of Health and Human Services under the Office of Inspector General, where you can also learn about the Medicare Fraud Strike Force.

Second is the incidence of suicide among physicians, often felt to be a result of so-called physician burnout due to conflicting imperatives of patient care, hospital requirements, insurer issues, and the needs of the physician herself.

You can learn more about both these issues online.

# Acknowledgments

Writing and publishing my first book, Wrongful Acts, fulfilled a long-time goal, with the storyline based in reality and well developed over the years, and where you can learn more about my characters Megan and Allysin McLoren, if you haven't already read it.

The positive response from readers to that book, and the many subsequent requests for another, especially if featuring those two characters, prompted me to consider writing this second book. I want to thank all my readers for that support and encouragement. Of course, it required an entirely new premise and plot, again drawing on my career as a physician and hospital medical director to fashion a story which would not only be readable, but also based in reality. Avoidable Harm fulfills that latter goal, as mentioned in my author note.

As with my first book, thanks to Susan Sutphin, who again provided an excellent editorial review and recommendations to enhance the narrative.

I'm also thankful for the continued support and encouragement of two established thriller writers in their own right, Jon Land and Jeff Ayres, along with their colleagues and staff at Thriller-Fest, the annual conference for suspense and thriller writers, which together have provided me with both ideas and motivation to continue writing.

On a technical note, thanks again to the staff at ebook launch who delivered an exceptional book cover that sets the tone of the story, and expert interior formatting for publishing.

And most importantly, my deep appreciation to my entire family for their collective support of my newfound writing journey: Andrew, Gregory, and especially Nicole, who continues to be my go-to for all editorial and publishing questions.

And to my wife, Alexis, thanks for supporting this writing journey, being my social media marketer and community publicist, and especially as a never-ending source of positivity to counter my insecurities!

# About the Author

Tony (Anthony) Sclama is a retired physician with an additional degree in healthcare management.

A Rhode Island native, his medical career spanned

thirty-two years, including a full-time practice of Urologic Surgery, and service as Chief Medical Officer at a community hospital in Baltimore, Maryland. He and his wife currently reside in Bethany Beach, Delaware, where he began his "second career" in writing suspense/thriller novels featuring backgrounds in medical and scientific issues.

His first book, Wrongful Acts, involves gene therapy, genetic engineering, and a conspiracy to defraud the FDA.

Follow Tony at www.tonysclama.com and on Facebook at Tony Sclama, Author.